A Candlelight Ecstasy Romance ®

"STAY WITH ME.
MAKE LOVE WITH ME AGAIN! . . ."

He began kissing her throat, his lips heated and moist. "The way you looked at me tonight . . . I know you want me. Show me! I've been aching to touch you all night. . . ."

He brought his mouth close to hers. His caresses had mesmerized her. She wanted to turn her face away but couldn't. His mouth fastened on her parted lips with obstinate passion as though he would never again release her. The breath was forced from her lungs. She was like a frail reed in his arms. . . .

A CANDLELIGHT ECSTASY ROMANCE ®

TO HAVE
AND TO HOLD

Lori Herter

A CANDLELIGHT ECSTASY ROMANCE ®

Published by
Dell Publishing Co., Inc.
1 Dag Hammarskjold Plaza
New York, New York 10017

Dell ® TM 681510, Dell Publishing Co., Inc.

Candlelight Ecstasy Romance®, 1,203,540, is a registered
trademark of Dell Publishing Co., Inc., New York, New
York.

ISBN: 0–440–18861–X

Printed in the United States of America
First printing—February 1983

*To my husband, Jerry
for his patience
and constant encouragement*

To Our Readers:

We have been delighted with your enthusiastic response to Candlelight Ecstasy Romances®, and we thank you for the interest you have shown in this exciting series.

In the upcoming months we will continue to present the distinctive sensuous love stories you have come to expect only from Ecstasy. We look forward to bringing you many more books from your favorite authors and also, the very finest work from new authors of contemporary romantic fiction.

As always, we are striving to present the unique absorbing love stories that you enjoy most—books that are more than ordinary romance.

Your suggestions and comments are always welcome. Please write to us at the address below.

Sincerely,

The Editors
Candlelight Romances
1 Dag Hammarskjold Plaza
New York, New York 10017

CHAPTER ONE

"Well, Ms. Smythe," Ben Hackett said, emphasizing the *Ms.* in his usual way, "you made the cover again." With unconcealed pride, he held up a sample of the next issue of *American Traveler* magazine.

Bald, overweight, and nearing sixty, he was sitting behind the cluttered desk in his office, observing the mildly startled expression of the young woman standing in front of him.

"Again? Three months in a row?" Her clear soft voice revealed some astonishment. "Well! So when do I get my raise?" she quipped, her green eyes carrying an impish sparkle as she took the cover from his hand.

Ben's gravel voice took on an impatient rumble. "It's coming, it's coming. You're not starving as it is."

"I'm just joking, Ben. Don't get your blood pressure up. So they're making the Everglades piece the lead article this month?"

"Yes, thanks to your outstanding photographs. That cover shot really wowed the art department. It'll be a great attention getter on the magazine stands, looking up that alligator's long wet snout into his beady eyes. How far away from him were you?"

She handed the cover back to him. "About six feet."

"Stacie! What did I tell you about taking chances like that?"

She shrugged and gazed out the large window behind him over the soot-darkened buildings of New York City. "He must have just eaten; he looked too lazy to move. It wasn't dangerous."

"Are you a zoologist that you can make determinations like that?" he asked severely. "You're a good photographer, Stacie, and I'd like to keep you in one piece. You practically drowned taking pictures in that storm on Lake Superior two years ago. Then you got lost for two days in the Nebraska grasslands. You even let yourself nearly freeze to death running around New York last winter taking pictures of our big snow storm. What are you trying to prove?"

"Nothing. I just want to get good dramatic shots. One has to be in the right place at the right time to get them. What's wrong with having a sense of adventure? It lets me know I'm alive. You'd probably admire that quality in a man," she said, a challenge in her tone.

"I wouldn't admire a man without common sense, which is what I suspect your problem is. Don't you know you're alive without putting yourself into such dangerous situations?"

Stacie looked down and didn't answer.

Ben made an exasperated sigh and looked at the cover photo again. "You do take great pictures, though. That background sunset over the swamp water creates just the right eerie effect." He shook his head. "I have an easy to use One Step, and I can't even get a decent snapshot of my granddaughter."

Stacie smiled and brushed aside a strand of her wavy auburn-brown hair. "I wish I could write like you," she said, returning his compliment. "That's why you're such a good editor. You can improve any article handed to you, even work from the best writers."

Ben folded his arms over his expansive stomach and eyed her with a speculative look, but she could see the humor lurking behind his narrowed eyes. "Go on. Flattery will get you everywhere," he said darkly.

"I'm not trying to flatter—"

"No," he interrupted, putting a touch of the hunted fox in his tone. "You're after my job! I can see the handwriting on the wall. Those pretty little wheels under that curly mop of yours are calculating that I'll retire in a few years, and you want to be ready to take over. That's why you've been asking me to look over all your writing efforts. Being the magazine's best photographer isn't enough for you? . . ."

Stacie knew well that he was joking, but she drew her brows together and tilted her head as she asked, "What's brought this on?"

Sighing heavily—Stacie knew it was for effect—he leaned to one side and pulled a thin manuscript out of his drawer. "Because I've just read this." He tossed it down on the desk. "It's flawless."

She leaned forward to see the print and recognized the article she had written on the Everglades. Stacie had begun a habit over the past year of doing her own story for each assignment on which she was sent as a photographer. It was the staff writers that she accompanied whose articles were actually published, of course, but she was often disappointed with their efforts. Many times she had thought they overlooked important points that were clearly illustrated in her photographs.

After some time as a staff photographer, she had developed the confidence in herself to believe that she could learn to write at least as well as they. Ben Hackett, the tireless man who virtually put together each issue of *American Traveler* from start to finish, had hired her over two years ago as a photographer. Since then he had also become her friend and career advisor. He knew of her aspirations to write and had been kind enough to offer criticism on her practice attempts.

"You liked it?"

"It's even better than the article I got from Larsen," Ben told her, referring to the writer she had accompanied to the Everglades. "Unfortunately, I'm going to have to use his since he's getting paid for it and I don't want to bruise any egos. But, since your writing has improved so much . . ." He paused as though firming some plan in his mind.

"Yes?" she said, eyes sharp and expectant.

"Well, Ms. Smythe, on the next assignment, I want you to not only take the photos, but do the necessary interviews and write the article too."

A broad, totally contented smile radiated from her face. "Thank you, Ben. I appreciate your confidence. In fact, I . . . I'm speechless."

He snickered softly. "With a mind as quick as yours, that won't last long. Sit down."

Stacie's lips compressed into an amused smirk. She drew up a metal chair and sat in front of his desk.

"Every once in a while I wonder," he continued as he pulled out some files and notes, "whatever happened to that shy, wide-eyed creature with the long, flowing hair who walked into my office two and a half years ago? It can't possibly have been the same Stacie Smythe we've all come to know and tolerate today," he said in a sarcastic mumble.

She took in this quip with a steady, steely smile. "Yes, I know how some men adore a cute, well-behaved little girl," she said in measured tones. "But if I've learned anything in my twenty-five years, it's that the little girl would serve herself better by growing up."

Ben raised his puffy eyes from his notes and stared at her. "You're in an especially gritty mood today."

She lowered her eyes from his a bit. "Sorry. I guess you happened to touch a sore point. I didn't mean to get on a soap-box."

The editor smiled a little. "A sore point? Ghosts from your silent past?"

Stacie responded with a knowing chuckle. Since she said very little about her private life, even refusing to give anyone a firm answer about her marital status, she knew there was always speculation about her among her co-workers. She sensed most assumed she was single since she lived alone. But she knew everyone at the headquarters of *American Traveler,* including Ben, would love to find out if such a self-sufficient young woman had a man in her life. "Maybe," she answered Ben's nudging question.

He looked over her delicate facial features framed by a halo of haphazard, dark curls, then shook his head slightly, apparently admiring her impenetrability. "Okay, Ms. Smythe," he said, a nuance of resignation in his voice. "I'll tell you about your next assignment."

"Fine," she said, letting her tone indicate she was ready to get back to business.

"We haven't done much on the Southwest lately," he went on, turning in his creaking swivel chair to pick up a copy of a *National Geographic* which was lying on the credenza next to his desk. He had a page marked with a paper clip, and as he opened the magazine she could see its cover. When she recognized which issue it was, a paralyzing coldness went through her. A copy of the same issue lay hidden away in her apartment, and she knew what it contained.

"I was very intrigued by this article the *Geographic* did about a year ago on the re-excavation of Snaketown, the archaeological dig near Phoenix. Did you happen to read it?" Ben asked.

Stacie swallowed before answering. "Yes."

"Good. Well, I don't want to do a carbon of their article, of course. But before telling you what I want," he said, twisting in his chair again to extract a typewritten letter from the confusion of papers on the credenza, "let me read you this. I think you'll be interested."

After pausing to put on his glasses, he read: " 'Dear Mr. Hackett, Thank you for your recent letter requesting permission from our Archaeology Department here at the university to use our facilities and interview certain of our staff for a proposed article for your magazine. Be assured we shall be happy to assist you in any way we can. We are still gathering a great deal of information from Snaketown, but if, as your letter suggests, you do prefer to center your article on another dig, we will help you sift through other possibilities.

" 'In leafing through the sample copy of *American Traveler* you sent me, I was pleasantly surprised to find that one of our former students is a member of your staff. In fact, it was one of Stacie Smythe's photos on the cover. She is a graduate of our university, as you probably know, and even took a few archaeology courses. I first met her when she was a student in one of my classes and became further acquainted with her during her senior year.

" 'Of course we will be happy to work with any member of your magazine's staff, but I for one would be particularly pleased to see Stacie again. Sincerely, Laurence Wilmott, Ph.D., Chairman, Department of Archaeology.' "

With a smile Ben took off his glasses and looked at Stacie. "How about that? You must have been a favorite down at the old Archaeology Department!"

Stacie could feel tears starting in her eyes, and it was only with a great deal of difficulty that she managed to speak in what resembled a normal tone of voice. "Yes, I remember Dr. Wilmott," she said softly with a small nostalgic smile. "He had just been made department head when . . . well, when I left. He's an older man; the gentlemanly type." She took a shallow breath and added in a near whisper, "He was always very kind to me," a nuance in her tone suggesting that there perhaps was some reason why he might not have been. "So this assignment will take me back to Phoenix?" she said in a stronger voice, hiding the shaking hands in her lap.

"I wouldn't want to disappoint Dr. Wilmott," Ben said jovially. "Actually, I had been thinking of sending Larsen. He did a piece on Mesa Verde for us a few years ago. I didn't realize you had taken any archaeology . . ."

"I had only two classes, that's all. By now I'm sure I've forgotten what I learned. Maybe Larsen would be a better choice," Stacie said with newfound energy, her hands twisting anxiously.

"No, no, you'll do just as good a job as he. Knowing the university staff will be an advantage, and you already have some familiarity with the area and the subject. It'll be a good first writing assignment for you."

After a long pause she said, "Yes, I suppose that's true," trying to imitate her usual confident manner. "What . . . what exactly did you want me to cover?" In spite of her pretense of self-possession, her heart began pounding with apprehension as she waited for his answer.

"Well, this *Geographic* article," he said, picking up the yellow-bordered magazine again, "touched on a theory espoused by a Dr. . . ." He paused to put on his glasses, then turned a page in the *Geographic* and ran his finger under the caption of one of the magazine's color photographs. Though from Stacie's vantage point the magazine was upside down, she could still make out which photograph he was checking. She closed her eyes tightly, not wanting to hear his next words.

"Here . . ." Ben continued, ". . . a Dr. Grayson Pierce. He's done a lot of research on the theory that some of the ancient Indians who built the prehistoric settlements in the Southwest, including Snaketown, may have migrated up from Mexico. He thinks there's quite a bit of evidence that shows a tie with the Mesoamerican cultures—you know, like the Aztecs, Mayas. . . ."

Oh, please, no! she barely kept herself from crying aloud. Desperate to keep control of herself and the situation, she mentally pulled herself together as best she could. "Look, if you're wanting me to do some follow-up on his theories, let me tell you I know for a fact that many experts disagree with him."

Ben looked up, his eyes puzzled and growing irritated. "Well that's okay," he said impatiently, as if trying to lessen her anxiety about the assignment. "The *Geographic* mentioned that too. You can cover both sides of the argument if you want."

Nervously she wet her lips. "But, what I mean is . . . why do a story on an unproved theory?"

Her editor seemed mystified by her objections. "Why not?" he argued. "It's just the type of thing our magazine does best. We don't go in for facts and reality so much as the *Geographic* does. Our magazine has the edge with armchair travelers who want a more romantic view of the world. And this Dr. Pierce's ideas are just the type of thing to capture our readers' imaginations. The thought that some of the ancient ruins in Arizona may have been built by cousins of the Aztecs is an intriguing notion."

Stacie felt desperate. "But . . . but if it's already been covered by the *Geographic* . . ."

Ben was clearly annoyed. "You read their article. It was mainly about Snaketown. They only *mentioned* Dr. Pierce's theory. I want you to do an in-depth report on the *theory*, making it sound as intriguing as possible, with a lot of good pictures of the ruins."

"Snaketown is one of the least photogenic places on earth!" she snapped.

"I know that, Stacie. I could tell by these photos that it's no Mesa Verde. That's why I mentioned in my letter to Dr. Wilmott that we want to find another dig if we can. When you interview Dr. Pierce, maybe he can suggest a more picturesque ruin to illustrate his theory. Okay?"

Interview Gray Pierce! she thought with seething irony. *What a farce that would be!* Stacie said nothing while her mind scrambled to find another plausible objection.

Ben noted her tense features. "What's the matter? Don't you like the climate in Phoenix or something? I thought you'd like to see some of your old friends again. Dr. Wilmott's eager to see you."

I wonder why? Stacie was thinking.

"Do you know Dr. Pierce?" Ben asked.

She glanced up sharply, then fought to control the tide of emotion rising inside her. She had kept her past a secret this long. After years of professionalism on the job, she didn't want to appear weak and emotional now. She had already argued too much. Ben was probably thinking she was more skittish than she ought to be about the writing assignment. She didn't want to blow this chance he had given her.

No, she couldn't let the past interfere. She had made her choice long ago and now her career was her life. If it meant she would have to see Gray again, then she would handle it somehow.

"Yes. Yes, I . . . took one of his classes."

"Well, that's great! This assignment should be a piece of cake, Stacie. Don't worry about it. And try not to get sunstroke or fall off a cliff!"

"I won't," she said, forcing herself to smile. "You're right, Ben. A piece of cake."

Home alone in her apartment that night, Stacie resolutely dug out the copy of the *National Geographic* she had hidden from her own sight at the bottom of a closet. She turned to the article on Snaketown and then found the picture Ben had referred to.

It was on the upper right hand corner of the page, an ordinary enough photo to find in the *Geographic*. It merely showed an archaeologist, a man in his late thirties, leaning against a partly seen vehicle, probably a Jeep, examining the markings on an ancient pot he held in his hands. He was wearing worn, dusty clothes made of rugged denim, and a western-style hat partly shaded his tanned face from the Arizona sun.

But though the photo was not unusual, there was something unusually arresting about the man himself. He appeared to be tall, lean, square-shouldered, undeniably handsome. Yet it was more than just his outward appearance. There was a brooding quality about him that could be seen in his pensive countenance, in the meditative attitude of his inclined head, in the angular passivity of his pose. He seemed a studious enigma, as though deep in his past lay some personal tragedy that had permanently sequestered his natural spontaneity. A feminine mind would intuitively know that to try to decipher such a man could be immediately addictive.

Stacie was well acquainted with his intriguing self-possession.

It was the very thing that had devastated her four years ago, the moment she first laid eyes on Gray Pierce. When she had known him better after a time, it seemed to her his brooding aspect had somewhat disappeared. Perhaps familiarity had made her indifferent to it. But after years of not seeing him, the picture in the *Geographic* had shown her that he still had that quality that in her youth had made her so weak-headed. It was why the magazine had lain in her closet for the past year, out of sight. She didn't want to be reminded.

And there was something else she had been startled to see, when she had first sustained the shock of coming across his photo in the magazine. On the third finger of his left hand could be seen, softly shining, a gold wedding band.

Looking at the picture, she wondered even now, why on earth, why in heaven's name was he still wearing that? Stacie had a duplicate of that ring to fit her own finger, but she had long ago forsaken it. It lay in a corner of her drawer, wrapped in a handkerchief; put aside but never quite forgotten.

CHAPTER TWO

"Dr. Wilmott!" Stacie exclaimed with surprise and a broad smile as she saw the professor's wiry frame approaching her at the airport. She had just stepped off the plane and was carrying a tote bag which held her camera and equipment. She blinked back unexpected tears as he took her free hand, cold with apprehension, in both of his. "It's wonderful to see you!" she said. "But I told you you shouldn't come to pick me up."

Dr. Wilmott smiled eagerly, his pale blue eyes brightening behind his thin tortoiseshell glasses. "Nonsense! It's no trouble at all. I couldn't have you return to Phoenix with no one to meet you and welcome you back."

"Thank you." His unsought and unexpected kindness was too much for her anxiety-ridden mental state, and emotion choked her words a bit. He had always been warm and pleasant in a scholarly, fatherlike way. He had been her favorite professor, next to Gray, when she was a student at the university. And now, it was reassuring to know that someone in Phoenix was glad to see her again.

Still smiling, he paused a moment to look at her, eyeing her hair and her jeans and turquoise blouse. "You've changed a little since we saw you last. You're even prettier."

"Thanks! You haven't changed at all." His steel-gray hair, thin face, and quietly perceptive eyes were just as she remembered.

"No, I guess I'll never be any prettier," he said jovially. He took the tote bag from her and they began to walk toward the luggage terminal. "I was really glad to get your call the other day, about flying out here to do the article. I was hoping things would work out that way."

"I know. My boss read me your letter." She wanted to know why he had indicated so much interest in having her come, but felt diffident about asking if Gray had anything to do with it. "So . . . how are things at the university?"

"About the same. Our department has been busy with the re-excavation of Snaketown for the last couple of years. We have new techniques now that. . . ." He checked his monologue and smiled. "Well, I don't want to get started on all that. I'd like to get reacquainted with you first, Stacie. I don't know what your plans are for today, but do you think you can fit lunch into them?"

His suggestion took her a bit by surprise. "I guess I ought to eat," she said, though she didn't feel very hungry. "All right, that would be nice. What I have to do, though, is get a rental car before I leave the airport."

"You needn't. My daughter is studying in Europe for a year, so you can borrow her VW."

"Thank you," she said sincerely, "but I couldn't. *American Traveler* pays for the rental car anyway."

"Well, this would save you all that paperwork, and I'm sure your magazine won't mind saving the expense. Now what else do you have to do?"

Stacie smiled at his insistent hospitality and decided to take up the issue of the rental car again later on. "Uhm . . . I have to find the condominium the magazine arranged for me to use. Then I was hoping to visit the Archaeology Department briefly to get the ball rolling on my article."

She told him this matter-of-factly as though this were just

22

another work assignment. All during the plane flight she had been drilling herself to look at the situation that way, hoping to talk herself out of her increasing edginess. With the reality of landing in Phoenix, she was now finding the method hadn't worked well at all.

"Sounds fine. But lunch first!" Dr. Wilmott said as Stacie spotted her luggage coming down the ramp.

He took her to a hotel coffee shop nearby. After they had ordered and were brought glasses of burgundy, an unrelaxed silence descended on their corner booth. Neither had mentioned Gray yet, and Stacie knew he was on Dr. Wilmott's mind as well as hers. Dr. Wilmott was one of the few people who knew of her marriage to Gray. Sensing her old professor was too polite to bring up the subject, Stacie knew it was up to her. Her expression determinedly stoic, she looked across the table at him, her heart pounding.

"What . . . what did Gray say when you told him I was coming?"

Dr. Wilmott seemed rather startled. "I didn't say anything to him about it, Stacie. I didn't know if you were still in touch with him or not and decided to let things take their own course."

Stacie felt numb suddenly, and her gaze slowly drifted toward her place mat. His reply was something of a shock, for somehow she had assumed that Gray would be prepared for her reappearance. It disturbed her that she would be taking him unaware, for it made his reaction even less predictable.

"Does he ever mention me?" she asked without raising her eyes.

Dr. Wilmott's voice was kind but truthful. "No, Stacie, he doesn't. Gray has always been a very closed person. I've known him for many years, but he never confides in me. It was a long while before I even suspected you weren't with him anymore. I noticed he had stopped mentioning you; and after a while, from a few things he happened to say, I deduced he was living alone again. I never knew you had gone to New York until your editor

23

wrote me and sent along that magazine with your photographs in it."

Stacie nodded her head. "I see." So that was how it was. She chuckled in a humorless way. "Gray must not have changed much. I never could figure him out either."

The head of the Archaeology Department looked at her with a slight puzzled smile. "How did you come to marry him, then?" He quickly became apologetic. "You'll forgive my curiosity, I hope; but when I learned of your marriage, I did sort of wonder how it happened."

The question seemed too much to answer in a few words. Stacie simply smiled and picked up her wineglass.

"I know you were in his class your last semester," he continued, his curiosity apparently compelling him on, "and I guess you two were married in the middle of it?"

Stacie swallowed a sip of wine and set the glass down, a grim smile on her face. "Yes, that's what happened. We ran off to Las Vegas. Can you believe that?" she asked with hard-edged amusement.

"That's right. I remember one of you telling me that much."

"I hardly remember the ceremony," she said, her thoughts drifting as she envisioned the scene in her mind. It had taken place in a small room somewhere. Both she and Gray were wearing blue jeans. She couldn't remember reciting the vows. All she could recall was that her hands were shaking, causing the small bouquet of flowers Gray had bought her to tremble in her fingers. She was so nervous that she thought the man marrying them must have assumed she was pregnant. Actually the situation had been quite the opposite. . . .

"It seems hard to imagine Gray eloping," Dr. Wilmott said, interrupting her brief reverie. "He doesn't seem the impulsive type."

"Oh, but he can be," Stacie assured him as their luncheon plates were brought to their table. "Impulsive and unpredictable."

24

She drank some more wine, then unenthusiastically dabbed a fork into her beef Stroganoff.

"So you knew each other only a month or two when you married?" Dr. Wilmott asked between bites.

"Not exactly," Stacie answered with some embarrassment. "Remember I was in your Level One Archaeology class the second semester of my junior year? Well, you were sick with the flu one day and Gray took over the class for you."

"I vaguely remember. That was when you first met?"

"Sort of." She began to laugh at her nebulous answers, feeling a little heady from the wine. "The whole story is so silly, when I think about it. You really want to hear it? No one ever told you?"

Wilmott shook his head. "Gray never gave me any details, and I was afraid you would think I was being judgmental if I questioned you about it. With Gray being your professor it was a ticklish situation."

"It sure was." As the major events of the story passed through her mind, she found herself looking at Dr. Wilmott with seeking eyes. "You have to understand," she said, stretching out her fingers toward him with gentle emphasis, "I was barely twenty-one and very naive. I had come to Phoenix to finish college—I'm from Joliet, Illinois, originally. I had had a terribly sheltered midwestern upbringing. And I was the dreamy type. I had this tendency all through high school and junior college to develop crushes on older men, usually my teachers. I don't know why, but fellows my own age always seemed so juvenile to me. They say girls mature faster; maybe that was the reason . . . though I certainly wasn't mature. . . ." Her mind wandered momentarily to a vision of her youthful self: a wide-eyed, frail girl with long hair floating down her back. She brought herself back to the present. "Anyway, that's how I was: romantic, inexperienced, always mooning about someone who was unavailable to me."

She took a long breath and smiled a little as she exhaled, suddenly feeling reticent about revealing so much of herself. Putting her elbow on the table, she pressed her forehead against

25

her fingertips for a few seconds. "It all seems so ridiculous now, I'm embarrassed to tell you about it."

Dr. Wilmott grinned reassuringly. "Everyone was young once. Go ahead—Gray took over my class . . ." he prompted her.

She sighed again. Why not tell him? She had purposely kept her mind off of Gray during the plane flight over, but damming up her thoughts had only made her more tense and nervous. Maybe it would be good to discuss it with someone, especially Dr. Wilmott, who knew them both and seemed sympathetic, though she wondered at his interest. Perhaps talking with him would help to dispel her anxiety about seeing her husband again. She didn't want to face Gray with her nerves as knotted and frayed as they were now.

"Okay," she said. "Yes, I . . . I was sitting in class with the other students waiting for you to come in . . ."

The first thing Stacie had noticed that afternoon in the large classroom was a quiet flurry of excitement among the female students. When she had looked up at the substitute professor who had entered the room she immediately knew why. Tall, lean, and muscular, his physique appeared flawlessly masculine; unsubdued by the conservative dark pants, tan corduroy jacket, and turtleneck he wore. He had slightly wavy brown hair, intelligent brown eyes, and a deep tan that indicated the number of hours he spent out of doors. But the most intriguing thing about him was the serious, almost brooding expression carried on his handsome, angular face. Stacie had noticed, as she silently observed him from her seat toward the middle of the room, that he smiled very little.

He paced leisurely back and forth as he lectured, his lean body moving with a careless, manly grace, his low voice sensually disturbing. Yet, though he exuded so much masculinity, he seemed totally unaware of his own attractiveness and oblivious to the electric reaction he was getting from the women in class. His whole mind and attitude seemed focused on the topic he was discussing and directed to presenting it in such a way that his students could grasp it.

He had, in fact, a remarkable gift for teaching and he was obviously dedicated. Even a few of the young men in class, who usually did nothing to hide their boredom, that day seemed almost fascinated by the lecture.

But Stacie, already half in love with his looks and mature bearing, couldn't help but wonder what this Dr. Pierce was like outside of class. Was he always so serious? Did he eat, sleep, and think archaeology? More to the point, did he have any women in his life, or did he make a habit of ignoring them? Did he live alone? She had visions of this breathtaking, brooding man going home at night to a quiet room to count potsherds.

This doubtful image was amended by the end of class when something happened which caused Stacie to completely lose her equilibrium. He had been telling his students that the ultimate goal of archaeology was to uncover and explain patterns of human behavior, in the hope of eventually devising laws of human behavior. This knowledge, he conjectured, could help man avoid past mistakes and might save the human race from possible self-destruction.

At this point one student raised his hand and philosophically asked, "Is man worth saving?"

For a moment the quiet professor had seemed taken aback by the question. But a shadow of a grin quickly appeared on his face and a certain glint came into his eye as he dryly replied, "Well, as a man I'd like to say I think *woman* is worth saving!"

While there was laughter and a sprinkling of applause from the rest of the class, Stacie stared at Dr. Pierce, wide-eyed and rather surprised. The old adage, "Still waters run deep," must be true, she was thinking. She was still smiling a bit when, suddenly, he turned his brown eyes directly on her. It was as though, unknown to her, he had singled her out earlier and now was looking for her reaction.

Stacie stopped breathing, her smile faded, and she stiffened as if in fear. The sudden knowledge that he was aware of her in

27

particular among a room full of students unnerved her. As if sensing her response, he self-consciously dropped his eyes and turned his head in another direction.

Stacie was finishing an abbreviated version of this story for Dr. Wilmott. Her gaze was faraway now, recalling that moment when her eyes had first met Gray's. How breathless and unknowing she had been, never dreaming what was to come of a harmless flirtation. She drew herself back to the present again and looked up at Dr. Wilmott. "So that was how we met," she said.

The head of the department chuckled. "I can just picture all the girls in class swooning over him. I've often noticed the reaction he gets from women, though he doesn't seem to care." He moved his coffee cup so the approaching waitress could pour him some more. "What happened after that?"

Stacie lowered her eyes with a smile that indicated embarrassment. "Oh, the story gets even more schoolgirlish."

Dr. Wilmott shrugged. "I'm enjoying it so far. Would you like some dessert?"

"No . . . well . . . okay," she answered, laughing at herself. "Why not? I didn't think I was so hungry."

After he had ordered them both a piece of fudge pie, she said, "I guess talking's good for me. I've never told anyone any of this."

"I won't repeat it. I hope I'm not prodding you into saying more than you wish," he asked her with concern.

"I don't mind, I guess. Though I'm curious why you're so interested."

The professor smiled. "My wife and I have been wondering about you two for the past couple of years. You seemed so happy when we had dinner at your house that time."

"We were happy then," she said softly. "It didn't last long." Looking up at him speculatively, she asked, "Are you hoping to play matchmaker and patch us back together again? Is that why you asked my editor to send *me* to do the article?"

Dr. Wilmott rubbed the side of his nose before he spoke. "I've always believed in seizing an opportunity. I had no idea how things stood between you two, but as my wife always says, you and Gray made an awfully charming couple. When I saw the possibility of bringing you two in close proximity again, I decided it was worth a try. I hope I haven't . . ."

"Gray knows nothing about this?" she interrupted him. "He didn't ask you to . . ."

"No, no. Believe me, he knows nothing about your coming, or even about the article. I figured what he didn't know wouldn't hurt him. Have I done wrong, Stacie, in trying to push you two together?"

"My editor might have sent me here anyway," she said with a shrug. "Maybe it's good. Maybe things will get settled."

"But . . . it's occurred to me that you may have met someone else. . . ."

She gave him a blunt, amused stare. "Me? No. Getting stung once is enough." She lowered her eyes. "Oh, I've had a few dinner dates now and then, but I've never met anyone I thought could . . ." She realized she was going to say "make me forget Gray." Suddenly she raised her eyes to Dr. Wilmott. "Has Gray . . . met anyone?"

Dr. Wilmott leaned back in his seat. "Not so far as I know. But of course he wouldn't have told me if he had. He usually has one or two awestruck college girls following him around, but he doesn't pay much attention."

Stacie gave a little groan and put her hand over her eyes. "Please! I was one of them."

Dr. Wilmott was amused by her reaction. After the waitress had brought their desserts, Stacie was prodded into continuing her story.

"Well, I asked around and found out he was single," she began, laughing at her youthful self. "I looked up his class schedule. I figured out that he always passed the library on his way back to his office at certain times, so I stationed myself there a lot, pretending to study on the library's front steps. At first I thought he didn't notice me, but he had. I'd catch him glancing

at me and then looking away. One day I felt unusually bold
. . ."

When she had seen him look in her direction that day, she had
cast caution aside and smiled at Dr. Pierce. Immediately she was
sorry she had. His eyes narrowed on her in stern disapproval, as
if reminding her that he was a professor with a Ph.D. and above
flirting with giddy young co-eds.

So, having been made to feel very foolish and childish, she
ended her habit of waiting for him. She had been behaving like
a movie star groupie and had finally been made aware of it.

She told herself then that she had no chance with him, anyway. He *was* a professor, much older than she, and attractive
enough to have his pick of much more sophisticated women. She
never waited on the library steps again, and as a result did not
see him for several weeks.

Then one afternoon as she was coming out of the university's
bookstore, she saw him a few feet away, walking up the sidewalk
directly in front of her. He slowed his pace and his eyes brightened the moment he recognized her. He seemed happy, even
relieved, to see her again, and when he came up to her he paused
to look down into her face. Their eyes held each other's for a
silent instant, hers filled with wonder and his with joy. He had
missed her! She could see it in his face.

But quickly his expression changed. He seemed to catch himself. She watched the anger come into his face, a self-directed
censure of his own lack of discretion. Resolutely lowering his
eyes, he quickly moved past her.

Stacie walked on and did not turn around. She moved as if in
a daze, for realization of the truth had come to her: He *was*
attracted to her! Very much attracted, she was certain. The fact
of it took her breath away.

Now, in the restaurant, as she recalled the fateful import of
that realization, she was reminded how the fact that this man

wanted her had suddenly made her feel like a woman and not a girl. She swallowed and continued the story to Dr. Wilmott.

"But I also recognized that he didn't want to be attracted to me. I could understand why he didn't want to start anything. There might have been trouble with the university. He probably didn't want to risk getting reprimands over a passing infatuation with a student. So, with much regret, I decided it was best to leave well enough alone. I was too shy to chase him in earnest, anyway. I told myself I was being very mature about it."

"I imagine you were," Dr. Wilmott said. "So you left well enough alone, as you put it?"

"Obviously not," said Stacie, shaking her head ruefully. "Summer came. I heard he went to Mexico. I stayed on campus and continued my studies in photography and journalism. I started sending some of my photos to magazines. *Arizona Highways* bought a few, and with that success I decided for certain what I wanted my career to be. Then the fall semester started, and I knew he was back on campus, but I didn't seek him out. At the end of that term I was filling out my schedule for my final semester. After choosing my other classes I realized I needed a fourth subject to meet the necessary number of hours to graduate. I had taken everything else I needed, so I decided to choose something for fun.

"I saw that Dr. Gray Pierce was offering a class called the Archaeology of the Southwest. I thought about my old infatuation with him. I hadn't seen him for many months and was beginning to think it was just a silly crush. How could anyone have been as attractive and elusive as I had made him out to be? I figured I must have grown up a lot since then. The class sounded interesting and I considered myself immune to whatever appeal he'd had for me the year before."

She chuckled softly. "Well, that was the fatal mistake. As soon as I saw him in class I realized it too."

In her mind she recalled the fleeting look of helplessness in Gray's eyes when he had first seen her that day. He hadn't known her name and didn't expect to find her there.

31

She also recalled her own reaction, her sudden realization that he was everything she had remembered. His masculinity, maturity, and self-definition were real and compelling. He still had that mysterious brooding quality that had fascinated her so. She had wanted to know him, understand him, break through that impenetrability to learn what he really was.

Her inner self churning now with recollected emotions, Stacie's expression grew morose and a feeling of hopelessness came over her. How could she have been so naive to think that she could ever really understand Gray?

"What happened?" Dr. Wilmott asked.

His voice broke her trance. She pulled her thoughts together. "Not much at first. There was just a growing uneasiness between us during class, the constant attempts to avoid eye contact. Soon I was wishing I could drop the course, but I needed the credits to graduate and it was too late to sign up for something else. As the weeks went on, one thing led to another. . . ."

As she reviewed the next sequence of events in her mind, Stacie quickly decided to skip parts of her story, feeling squeamish about telling Dr. Wilmott some of the more intimate details —like the day she had stayed after class to see Gray for a moment. . . .

"I'll have to miss Friday's class, Dr. Pierce," she had told him in an unsteady voice. He was erasing the blackboard with his left hand. His profile looked stern and remote.

He immediately turned toward her, and she noticed for the first time at close range the amber highlights that gave warmth to his brown eyes, in spite of his reserved demeanor.

"I want to leave for Monument Valley that day to do an assignment for my photography class," she explained, shyly looking to the floor.

"All right," he said and went back to his erasing. "You're a photographer?"

"Yes," she said, her lips forming a trembling little smile.

He nodded his head slightly, and she thought she saw a hint

of amusement in his face as he put down the eraser and picked up his textbook from the instructor's desk. He began to move past her toward the door, and his open jacket brushed her arm as he did so. It was only a slight physical contact with his tall frame, but it swept away all her composure and left her suddenly weak.

He turned around, saw her shaken appearance, and took a step back to her. "I'm sorry, did I bump you?"

"No, it . . . it was my fault." she said breathlessly.

After eyeing her seriously for several moments, he set his book back on the desk and said, "Miss Smythe, I think we need to discuss something." He paused, looking down at the ground as she waited apprehensively. "Maybe I'm imagining it, but . . . you seem to have a crush on me." He looked up to see her shrink away from him against the blackboard. Her face went hot and she wished she could run away.

"I don't say this to embarrass you, really I don't," he hurried to assure her. "In fact, it's been . . ." he paused a long while as if unable to find the right word, " . . . rather flattering for me. But I think you must sense as well as I that it's making things difficult for us . . . for us . . ." He left off in some confusion, as if his words were taking him in a different direction than he intended.

"Yes, I know. I'm sorry," Stacie whispered, unable to take her eyes off the floor. "I didn't mean to cause a problem."

"It's not your fault. I had crushes when I was young too. But, if you could just not look at me the way you do. . . ."

"I try not to look at you," she blurted out. "I don't mean to distract you."

"But you do!" he said sharply. "You sit there with those big eyes, beautiful hair falling around your neck and shoulders . . ."

Abruptly she looked up at him and found his eyes following a long, thick lock of dark hair as it trailed innocently down her blouse toward the soft rise of her breast. His eyes slid up to hers and she stared back at him, her breath caught in her throat.

An intense inner struggle showed in his darkening eyes. "Yes, it's my fault too," he admitted in a harsh, hushed voice. "We're both of us very foolish, Stacie! This can't go on. The university takes a dim view of professors who exchange A's for favors from their women students."

"I'm not . . ."

"I know that's not what you're up to. You don't *know* what you're doing. But that's how everyone else would see it."

"But nothing's happened."

He stared at her fixedly. "It may . . . if we aren't careful."

Stacie's eyes widened in alarm at the implication of his words.

His eyes flashed. "Yes I want you to," he growled, keeping his voice low and glancing toward the open door. "You're so naive you don't know that you've been playing with fire!" He closed his eyes and shook his head impatiently. "Why am I telling you this? I should never have said anything to you. I should have just walked out. Now you see this . . . this attraction is mutual. I didn't want you to know."

"I guessed it," she said softly, looking up into his face.

His eyes opened in a hard stare. "Did you. Well, it can't go any further! You understand, Stacie? It's no good. Even if I weren't your professor, it wouldn't work. You're so much younger than I, and more naive than you ought to be."

She felt hurt and indignant. "I'll try to behave with more decorum," she said tensely.

He reached out and placed his hand over her bare forearm. "I'm not blaming you. If the circumstances were different . . . if I weren't a professor and . . ."

"And I weren't such a child!" she finished in a cutting tone, wrenching her arm from his warm, gentle fingers.

"Stacie," he said comfortingly, reaching to touch her again, "I didn't mean that you weren't desirable. . . ." He stopped short and released his hold on her upper arm as if he had unknowingly clasped something very hot. Wrath filled his eyes. "No, you're no child. There's a woman beneath that innocent exterior mak-

34

ing me say and do things I don't want to and never thought I would! I think you'd better go now."

"Yes," she whispered, bowing her head. She turned and walked out of the room without looking back, but could feel his eyes upon her. Yes, she understood his position and the circumstances but didn't know whether to respect him or curse him for doing the proper thing. The touch of his fingers on her skin lingered with her, making her feel sensual and vulnerable and giving her an intense yearning to know what deeper sensations his hands, voice, and lips could provoke.

Stacie had strictly avoided meeting his eyes during class for the next few weeks and did not speak to him at all. She began to assume there would be no further encounters between them, until the time midterms came. Then, as she was sitting at her desk writing the test, she happened to look up and found him staring at her. The deep, urgent longing in his eyes unnerved her and her pulses began to race. His gaze held hers for some time until, as if in pain, he slowly drew his eyes away and opened up a book in front of him. Stacie finished the test hardly knowing what she was writing.

At the next class he gave the specifications for the term paper he wanted written and asked each student to see him in his office for individual consultation about the choice of topic.

Stacie was rather stunned. Did that include her? Would he really want to see *her* alone in his office?

Two days later, in the middle of a long, languid, spring afternoon, she found herself hesitating at the threshold of the open door of his office.

It was a small room, filled with bookshelves and file cabinets. A wooden desk was against the side wall, and he was sitting there working on some papers. His jacket was hanging over the back of his chair, and his shirt sleeves were rolled up, revealing strong, tanned forearms. She studied his profile for a moment before clearing her throat softly and on purpose.

He turned his head. "Stacie," he said with a slight hesitance.

"I've come to discuss my term paper. You said you wanted everyone to. . . ."

"I remember what I said. Come in," he said quietly and with some amusement in his tone. He lowered his eyes as she dutifully stepped into the room. "Have a seat." He motioned to an empty chair next to his desk.

She did as he asked, then looked up to find him studying her. She was startled at first and on her guard. But he seemed composed; she found no hint of the longing she had encountered in his eyes during the midterm.

She knew she shouldn't be disappointed, but she was. It seemed he was regarding her now as any academic instructor might look upon a nervous young student—with patience and paternalistic amusement. Had he forgotten the things he had said the last time they had spoken?

They began to discuss her term paper. It was then that he first mentioned to her his theory of prehistoric links with Mexico. Stacie had listened, fascinated, as he explained the general concept and went on with a few anecdotes about the research work he had done in Mexico the previous summer. But soon she began to feel awkward and lowered her eyes to her lap. His talking to her so personally and so freely made her feel shy. It was as though they knew each other more closely than they actually did, and she didn't know how to react.

It seemed he had quickly become aware of his lapse, however, and his voice was reserved as he said, "I think the topic you've chosen is good. Now, if you have no further questions . . ."

"Are there any particular sources you can recommend?" she asked before he could finish.

He paused in thought. "The library has a good section on archaeology. And," he rose from his chair and went to a low bookshelf beneath the large window that brightened the room, "there's a chapter in here that should be useful for your topic." He handed her a thick book.

"Thank you," she said, taking it. She immediately noticed the name of the author. "You wrote this?" she asked in an awed voice.

He nodded curtly and with an impassive countenance. He was still standing, and she sensed he was silently cueing her that he wished her to leave. Feeling self-conscious again, she picked up the books and shoulder bag she had brought with her, thanked him once more and headed for the door.

But when she neared it, she heard his voice hesitantly say, "You . . . did well on your midterm."

She swung around to face him, her auburn hair bouncing lightly and then settling back softly over her shoulders. "I did?" she said happily, her green eyes large and shining.

"Yes," he answered very softly, his eyes suffused with a wistful expression that gradually changed, as he stared at her, to the ache of longing she had seen before.

Her heartbeat quickened. "I'd better go," she said breathlessly and turned to hurry out the open door.

"Stacie!"

She stopped. There was a low urgency in his voice that made her body grow taut with expectation and anxiety. "Yes?" she said without turning to face him. Suddenly she felt his strong hands on her upper arms, pulling her back from the threshold. He stepped past her, took a fraction of a second to check the empty hallway, then closed the door. Her eyes were wide with alarm as he turned to face her.

"It's no use, Stacie," he said in a quiet, defeated tone, but his eyes were bright and agitated. She took a small step back as he approached her. Gently taking the books she held in her arms from her, he tossed them onto the chair. He slipped his fingers beneath the strap of her shoulderbag and it dropped to the floor with a quiet thud.

"Dr. Pierce!" she softly exclaimed, a trace of f⸻ ᵻn her voice as she took another small step back.

"Gray. Call me Gray." He clasped her sʰ⸻ large hands and pulled her close to him, whiⸯ ardently over her face. "I've tried to ignor⸲

pretend you were just like any other student. It's no use; I can't! I promised myself that when you came about your term paper I would treat you just like the others, so you would see—and I could convince myself—that I was determined to overcome this thing between us."

He paused, shaking his head meaningfully while his fingers tightened their grip. "Then you walk in—beautiful, shy, sincere —flashing those innocent eyes at me. I have no more resistance, Stacie. I can't leave you alone! I won't!"

His arms came around her, crushing her against him, while his lips came down forcefully against hers. Stacie's reflexes momentarily resisted the sheer power of him, but then she relaxed and allowed her body to mold itself against his.

She felt enveloped by his masculine being, eager to experience his strength. When he finally drew away a bit, she shyly but urgently brought her arms up about his neck, wanting another kiss. If he was a little startled he did not argue, and quickly their lips were meeting again in a long, luxurious embrace. Eventually he slid his mouth from hers and spread a line of kisses over her cheek and chin, and down her delicate long neck. Her breath began coming in small shallow gasps as she writhed against him in flaming reaction to the sensations he was causing.

He pulled away from her and looked into her face, his own breathing ragged. "I never imagined you would be so responsive," he whispered, his lips close to hers, his breath mingling with hers. "We have to decide what we're going to do, Stacie."

Her eyes clouded woefully. "Don't say we can't see each other, Gray." She clutched the front of his shirt and clung to him. "Please don't tell me that again. Not now. Not after this."

His arms tightened around her. "I won't, Stacie. I couldn't. You're driving me wild," he said, his mouth against her hair. "I can't concentrate on anything anymore. Staying away from you doesn't work; but we can't meet like this. Maybe . . . can you see me for dinner tonight? Some place where we won't run into anyone we know. . . ."

* * *

"After a while we started dating secretly," Stacie summed up to Dr. Wilmott. "It was innocent enough at first. We'd meet at a restaurant and then he'd drive me back to the dorm. But finally I went with him to his house after dinner one evening, against his better judgment, I think. Things . . . well . . . got out of hand pretty quickly," she said, carefully choosing her words while shifting uneasily in her seat. Her face colored slightly. "You see, our attraction to one another was mainly physical, I'm afraid. At least that's the conclusion I've come to in the years since."

She drew her eyes away from Dr. Wilmott's understanding face and looked down, wondering for a moment if her conclusion had been correct. Dismissing the thought, she continued.

"Before things went too far that evening, he walked away from me and over to the window. He asked if I wanted to have an affair? I . . . didn't answer. He turned and looked at me and said, 'It isn't what *I* want for you. You're not the type to have a clandestine affair with your professor.'

"I asked what he suggested we do? He said, 'There's a solution, though we may be fools to take it.' Those were his exact words," Stacie said with irony.

"His solution was that we fly to Las Vegas that weekend and get married. I was astonished. That he would actually want to marry me was more than I had ever hoped for. I asked him why he wanted to? He hadn't told me he loved me, you see, and . . . I guess I was looking for that.

"He answered that he was afraid of taking advantage of my inexperience. And he was worried the university might think I was offering myself to him in exchange for a good grade. If anyone found out about us before I graduated, it would look better for both of us if we were married, he told me.

"Maybe you can imagine how disappointed I was with his answer," she told Dr. Wilmott with a sad smile. "It sounded so cut and dry, like he just felt guilty about me, and I told him so. I asked him point blank if he loved me?"

Stacie paused and made a dry chuckle, though her eyes looked glazed. "I'll always remember his reply," she said. She tried to swallow the lump forming in her throat. "It was the closest thing to a declaration I ever got from him. He said: 'I don't know. Why else would I have allowed my life and my professional routine to be disrupted so completely?'

"As he said it, I thought I heard a note of warmth and feeling in his voice, and I took it as a positive reply. But he never actually said to me, 'I love you, Stacie.' " She gave a little shrug and blinked hard. "At least he didn't lie."

"But Stacie," Dr. Wilmott interjected, "Gray isn't the type to express his feelings. Just because he didn't say the words doesn't mean he wasn't in love with you."

"Maybe," Stacie said. Her voice was strained with bottled up tears, but she wanted to continue the story and forced herself to go on, even though it was becoming painful. "But I think if he did love me, we would still be together. Although, I can't say he didn't warn me." She forced an empty little laugh. "I was getting all excited, you see, about the prospect of eloping with him. In fact I was to have an interview that weekend for a job as a photographer with a nature magazine in Denver. It could have been the start of my career. But I was so blind with infatuation and eager to marry Gray, I thought nothing of canceling it. All I wanted was Gray.

"So, as I was saying, he warned me to keep my feet on the ground. He told me: 'This is marriage we're talking about, not some weekend fling!' Then he listed all the pitfalls: I was very young and naive, and he was twelve years older than me. When I was more mature, I might decide that he wasn't the husband my adult self wanted. He added that our relationship might be just an intense infatuation that could fizzle out with time. He finished by saying that a statistician wouldn't give our marriage very good odds.

"I felt hurt and complained he wasn't being very romantic." She made a tremulous smile. A tear slid down her cheek as Gray's reply echoed through her head: "But you see, Stacie," he had said in a voice that was gentle, yet mildly ironic, "I *am* romantic. I tend to forget all these worries when I look in your eyes. And when you kiss me, I can't remember a damned thing."

She suddenly noticed the serious, empathetic look in Dr. Wilmott's eyes at seeing her tears. She sniffed and tried to laugh a bit. "I was very young then. I believed in romance and the happy ending. I know better now." Absently, she pushed away her half-eaten piece of pie as her eyes grew empty.

"So you flew off to Las Vegas that weekend?"

"Yes," she replied, wiping the last wetness from her cheek with her fingers. "I didn't want to arouse anyone's suspicions at the dorm, so I wore blue jeans, packed an overnight case, and told my roommate I was visiting a cousin. Gray bought our matching wedding rings in Las Vegas. He also bought me a small bouquet of flowers; very pretty—tea roses and baby's breath and . . . I forget what else. I lost it somehow after the ceremony. I never knew how. . . ." she said, her troubled eyes staring at her empty wineglass but not focused on it. She couldn't even hold on to the flowers he had given her. How could she have hoped to hold on to him? And just like the flowers, she had never known exactly how she had lost him. . . .

"Then you kept the marriage a secret until after you graduated," Dr. Wilmott prompted her to continue.

She looked up and her gaze refocused on his patient and intent eyes. "Yes. We didn't even tell my parents. I still lived at the dorm. We'd meet at his house on certain afternoons to . . ." She suddenly left off not knowing how to finish.

"I can fill in the blanks," Dr. Wilmott said with an understanding smile.

She blushed. She didn't need to be so self-conscious about it, she told herself. They were married at least. But all the trystlike secrecy had made it seem a little sinful—and made the lovemaking so terribly intense. She remembered those languid, sensual afternoons spent in Gray's arms, the two of them alone in his cool, quiet house, the bright sun streaming through the curtained window, bathing their bed in warm light. If only she could feel his strong body against hers once more! How often in the past years, living alone, had she thought of the treasured hours spent with him in lovemaking. . . .

A clatter of silverware at the booth in back of her returned her to the present with a start. She glanced up at Dr. Wilmott self-consciously, embarrassed at where her thoughts had led her. She was also angry with herself. She didn't need to remember her lonely nights now, just before she was going to see Gray again.

"Maybe we should go," she suggested.

Dr. Wilmott nodded. "I do have a class at three and we need to stop at your condominium. We can talk more on the way."

CHAPTER THREE

They left the restaurant and drove across town toward Scottsdale. It was a clear sunny day and growing very warm. "It feels like the middle of summer already, instead of June," she told Dr. Wilmott.

"I can tell you've been away. This is a typical spring day. We could use some rain though. Been awfully dry this year."

Stacie gazed down the long straight street as they moved along in the slow traffic. She remembered the first time she had seen Phoenix and how different she thought the city was from Joliet. Situated on flat ground with occasional low mountains like Camelback Mountain intruding on its grid pattern of streets, the sprawling city and its suburbs seemed to spread endlessly. There was a central cluster of very tall buildings surrounded by acre upon acre of small low buildings of varying ages and styles. Far from being compactly built, the metropolis took up two to three times as much space as a similarly populated urban area would in the Midwest or East.

How quiet it seemed now to Stacie. She had grown used to the hassles and energetic momentum of New York City. Here there was no feeling of being swallowed up in the cavernous streets between skyscrapers, no shouting matches between taxi drivers, no masses of people walking down broad sidewalks at all hours of the day. Phoenix seemed a relaxed town, not quite separated yet from its surrounding desert landscape and too sprawled and unplanned to be beautiful, but with a pace and life-style of its own. And, she thought to herself as she looked at the many expensive shopping centers and restaurants they were passing, not reticent about catering to its element of wealth and class.

"Are you and Gray still married then?" Dr. Wilmott asked after some minutes of silence between them.

"Legally. We're divorcing."

"When will the divorce be final?"

Stacie exhaled sharply. "We haven't even started proceedings yet. It was Gray's idea to divorce but getting him to attend to it is like pulling teeth. After a year went by and I heard nothing, I had a lawyer get in touch with him. Gray got an attorney, and, supposedly, he filed for divorce here in Phoenix. But when my lawyer flew out here and appeared before a judge, Gray's attorney informed them that Gray hadn't given him some necessary papers. A new date was set, and when that time came, his attorney didn't even show up. Since then I've just let it ride. It doesn't matter, I suppose, unless one of us wants to remarry. But I wish it were settled. I don't like having it hanging over my head, not knowing what he wants, never feeling quite free."

"An odd situation," Dr. Wilmott said. He was pulling up in front of a new two-story building, which had a mixture of Spanish and modern elements in its architectural style. Stacie saw the number on the building and realized this was her condominium.

"It looks nice, doesn't it?"

"Your magazine must want to keep you happy!" Dr. Wilmott said as he got out of the car. They collected her luggage and took it up to a second floor suite. Stacie found her key and opened the door to a beautifully furnished apartment which featured a view of the graceful slopes of Camelback Mountain.

Conscious of the lateness of the hour, Stacie left her camera case and luggage unopened after placing them in the bedroom. She did take a few minutes to freshen her makeup and check her hair. Looking at herself in the mirror, she wondered how Gray would react to her permanented hairstyle. She had always felt that the thing that had attracted him most was her long, luxuriously cascading hair. He was always touching it, stroking it, playfully tugging on stray locks. Sometimes he even brushed it for her. She remembered that he had once murmured, in an intimate moment, that he loved the way it fell over her shoulders and breasts.

Now it wasn't nearly so long, barely touching her collar, and what was left was a stylish mass of curls. If he didn't like it that was too bad, she told herself as she applied a little makeup. There was no reason to feel she should apologize to him for her appearance. She had wanted to look more sophisticated when she started working in New York, and now she did.

She walked into the living room and told Dr. Wilmott, who was sitting on the couch in front of the large window, that she was ready. He glanced at his watch.

"That was fast. We still have a few minutes. Do you mind if I ask one more prying question?"

She smiled and sat in the chair opposite him, across a large glass coffee table. "I guess not."

"What exactly led to your breakup with Gray? You seemed so happy together."

"My career," she answered. "We had been married about five months. After living at home with him for a while, I was beginning to get bored. Not with Gray, you understand, but with being a housewife. I had just graduated from college; I wanted to accomplish something, make my mark in the world. I kept sending my photographs, mostly Arizona landscapes, to various magazines. Gray knew I was doing this, but he never said much about it. I had the feeling he didn't like it.

"Well, one day Ben Hackett called from New York. He wanted to buy some of my photos of Monument Valley and offered me a free-lance job, accompanying one of the *American Traveler* writers to Mount McKinley National Park in Alaska. I was thrilled, but when I told Gray about it, the roof fell in. Gray

45

wouldn't hear of it. A woman's place is with her husband, he said. He didn't mind if I sold a few photos now and then, but he wouldn't stand for me galivanting around the country for weeks at a time with people he didn't know. He added that I was too inexperienced to even know how to get on a plane by myself."

She made a grim little chuckle. "It was the first time I truly began to realize that his treating me like a little girl was more than just a part of his protective, doting manner with me. He really wanted me to stay the childlike woman he had married. Finally, after a lot of arguing, he said he wouldn't permit me to go. *Permit* me!"

She stopped speaking and in her mind heard the echo of her long-ago reply: "I'm your wife, not your ten-year-old daughter! I don't need your permission!" The words had come from her mouth almost before she knew it. She remembered Gray's expression. His color changed and an odd, bleak look had crossed his face. His voice was strained. "Why should you want to go running around the country? Aren't . . . I thought you were happy. . . ."

"I am happy, but this is a chance at the career I've always wanted."

If he had seemed to fall apart for a moment, he had quickly pulled himself together. His voice grew stern. "That particular career and this marriage aren't going to mix, Stacie. Get some job here in Phoenix if you like, but you aren't flying off to Alaska or anywhere else. Not as long as you're married to me!"

After a few minutes of silence she had quietly asked, "How could you stop me?"

She remembered how he stared at her, his eyes still and looking as though they were made of glass. "You're right. I can't prevent you from leaving. But if you go, don't bother to come back. Do you understand?" His voice was low and articulate; the recollection of his tone put a chill through her.

"Are you all right? Is this too difficult for you to talk about?" she heard Dr. Wilmott's courteous voice say to her.

"What? No, I'm fine." She shook her shoulders slightly and straightened her back. "Remembering all the gory details is good for me. In fact I want to keep them in mind when I see Gray again," she said bitterly. "I don't want to get all pliant and weak-kneed if he should look at me kindly with those brown eyes of his."

Dr. Wilmott appeared saddened by her hard stance toward Gray, but made no comment. Instead he cued her to continue. "So, Gray said he wouldn't permit you to go . . ."

"Yes, he said if I couldn't stay home and be a decent wife to him, I could forget the marriage."

"Decent wife? He said *that*?" Dr. Wilmott asked, his tone sounding as though he was disappointed with Gray.

"According to him, a decent wife is one who's home with her husband every night. And if I ran off to pursue my 'precious career' as he put it, I'd better be prepared to pay the consequences."

"By that he meant he'd divorce you?" Dr. Wilmott asked.

"He didn't use that word then. In fact, he said he was trying to keep the marriage together, and preventing me from following my career was supposed to be for my good as well as his. But he finished by saying I'd have to choose between him and Alaska."

"And?"

"I chose Alaska. I thought he was bluffing. He'd said it so easily, I didn't think he meant it. I figured he was trying to manipulate me with threats and I decided I'd better make a stand. I was afraid giving in to him then would set a bad precedent for the future."

"So you went to Alaska?"

"For three weeks. I got some marvelous shots in the wilderness. The magazine was very pleased. I knew then that I had made the right decision. To stay home and live a cloistered existence might be fine for some women but not me. Though I admit Gray made it seem attractive. He was very attentive. A good husband, really, as long as I played the housewife role. In fact that was why I couldn't believe that he would actually separate from me. Sometimes I'd had the impression that he would have done anything, given me anything I wanted to keep me happy. It was like he had wrapped himself around my finger."

"That was my impression when I saw you together. He doted on you. I wouldn't have believed he could be that way unless I had seen it myself," Dr. Wilmott said.

"I know. It was such a shock to find he hadn't changed his mind. When I came back from Alaska I told him I had missed him very much but that I loved doing the assignment and hoped the magazine would give me another. He told me I'd better get a lawyer. And that was it."

"That's all he said?"

"Oh, it was another terrible argument. He said that I had changed and would never be content with him. I still don't know what he meant by that. I never made demands on him. I never wanted wealth or fame or anything like that. I just wanted to pursue a career like he pursued his. He seemed to overreact to the whole idea—said I sounded like some damned women's libber!"

"Did he offer any compromises?"

"No!" she said, her tone showing her sense of injustice. "I asked him, 'You don't even want to try to work things out?' He said, 'Why prolong the agony?' My bags were still packed from Alaska. I left that night and took a plane to New York."

Dr. Wilmott sighed and shook his head. "I can see I have my work cut out if I'm going to try to bring you two together again."

"Don't count on success," Stacie said dryly.

Dr. Wilmott eyed her seriously. "Would you like to patch up the marriage?"

Stacie's expression became confused. She actually had never decided what her feelings were on the question. Though conscious that she spent more time than she should pondering her memories of Gray, she wasn't sure that living with him again would solve anything. "I don't know. Not unless he's changed some of his attitudes; not unless I felt that he looked upon me as something more than a cute toy. No, I wouldn't go back to the same situation. But then, he might not want me anyway. I've changed a lot. I'm not the little girl he married."

"No, I can see you've grown very independent." He stood up. "Well, we'd better get along to the university now."

Stacie paled slightly. "Yes, of course." She rose from her seat and followed him out the door, all the while trying to suppress a sudden feeling of panic. She wondered if she really was as in charge of herself as she liked to think.

As they drove toward the university, Stacie grew increasingly anxious and jittery, not quite able to keep her hands from fidgeting with her blouse and her hair. Talking with Dr. Wilmott about Gray had had a calming effect for a while, but now her nervousness was returning in full force.

All at once Dr. Wilmott, who had been driving in thoughtful silence, spoke. She turned with a start.

"You know," he said, "your story about leaving Gray and flying to New York reminds me of something. It was some campus gossip I heard long ago and had almost forgotten. I don't know if it was true. About fifteen years ago when Gray was one of my students in graduate school, there was a story going around that he was in love with an undergraduate student. She was quite beautiful, I gathered, and aspired to be a model or actress. Something along that line. Talk was that Gray was hoping to marry her, but she wanted to go to New York to further her career first. She did go and met with some success. Meanwhile she kept stringing Gray along, promising to come back, but apparently she never did."

Stacie's eyes were wide as she stared at him, barely breathing. "He was in love with someone else before he met me?"

Dr. Wilmott smiled. "Well, Stacie, how old was he when he married you? Thirty-four? Did you really think he had never had any previous girl friends?"

"No, but I didn't know he had ever wanted to *marry* anyone else. I wonder if she left him for the same reason I did?"

49

"There are some interesting parallels. But as I say, I don't know how much of that story is true."

Still in shock over this revelation, Stacie ran a shaking hand across her forehead. "You've been a fountain of information this afternoon, Dr. Wilmott. I should have had this talk with you before I married him!"

He laughed. "Even if I had remembered the story then, I probably wouldn't have told you."

Recognizing familiar landmarks, Stacie knew they would be at the university in a matter of minutes. Though she would dearly have loved to ponder the tale of Gray's former amour and pumped Dr. Wilmott for any more shreds of information he might remember, she had to put it aside. Shortly she would see Gray, and she wanted to know what to expect.

"What's he like now? I mean, has he changed any in the last two and a half years?"

Dr. Wilmott let out a long, ponderous sigh. "That's a hard question. I'd have to say yes and no. He does his work and goes through his paces like he always did. But there's been a vacuousness about him lately, like his mind is always on the other side of the hill somewhere. I can't quite put my finger on it. I don't claim to ever have known what he thinks about, but I always had the impression his life revolved around his work. Now, sometimes I don't know if he's thinking at all."

Stacie was beginning to feel alarmed. "Is it serious, do you think?"

Dr. Wilmott chuckled. "No. I'm not about to have him put away yet. Sorry, I do have a tendency to exaggerate sometimes. He's all right; so far I can't complain about his work. It's just that I sense he's beginning to drift and I don't want that to happen. I have to confess, Stacie, that my bit of effort to get you here isn't entirely for altruistic reasons. I'd rather leave the matchmaking and reuniting of long lost lovers to my wife. My concern is for the Archaeology Department. It's been running beautifully, and the main reason has been Gray's dedication. He sets the example for the other staff members. I was planning to retire in a few years, and Gray would have been my natural successor as head of the department. But, if he begins to lose that dedication, then I'm not sure what will happen. I may have to work longer than I wanted to, and my wife won't be happy about that. And I . . . I'm saddened to sense Gray changing this way. I don't really understand him, but I've grown fond of him over the years."

Stacie took a long breath and let it out slowly. "And you're hoping *I* can remedy all that?"

"I don't know, but I thought it was worth a try. Seeing you again should shake him up a little. He's going to have to deal with you, pull his mind back to reality from wherever it is. He's about thirty-seven now, you know—the age when some men begin to wonder what they're living for. Putting you in front of him again may make him remember. He was happy with you once, Stacie."

"Maybe he'd rather *not* remember that. Maybe *I'd* rather not."

Dr. Wilmott had directed the car into a university parking lot and turned off the motor. He looked at Stacie, studying her fragile features, now tense with emotion, and her beautiful green eyes, their color intensified by a glaze of unshed tears. He turned slightly and put his arm over the seat back.

"Stacie, my opinion may not be worth much, and heaven knows Gray is a difficult man to fathom, but I don't think he's ever got over your leaving him."

"He wanted me to leave. He told me to," she argued, confused by Dr. Wilmott's perception of things.

"Gray, I think, is a person who is perfectly capable of wanting two opposing things at once. At any rate, Stacie, this marriage of yours is still unfinished. I'm hoping you won't give up the idea that it may still work."

CHAPTER FOUR

Stacie was feeling weak from nerves as she walked down the hall with Dr. Wilmott. On either side they were passing the offices of the Archaeology Department staff. Soon they came to a halt in front of Dr. Wilmott's door; Gray's was the next one down.

"I'm afraid I have to leave you now," Dr. Wilmott told her. "I have to give my class a test, but I'll be back in an hour. Gray should be in his office. Perhaps you can . . ."

"Yes, I'll see him," she said in a small, breathless voice.

"Good luck." He touched her arm reassuringly before going into his office. A moment later he left, carrying a briefcase. She watched him walk down the hall until he turned and disappeared from view. She looked for a few moments at the high ceilinged hallway of the old university building, so familiar to her from her own student days. She recalled other times in the years past when she had waited in this hallway to see Gray.

Before their marriage she had been terribly diffident about talking to him at all, because there was so much that was felt but unsaid lying between them. And then came the day when she had hesitantly come to his office to discuss her term paper, when he had suddenly closed the door and she was in his arms for the first time. Within weeks they were secretly married. After that when she visited his office, it was a matter of playacting, of pretending to be just his student when in fact she had become his lover. She had never stood in this hall waiting to see him without having some concern over how she should behave, and today was worst of all. Today she had no idea what to say to him or how to say it, whether she should be distant or cordial. She didn't even know for certain what their relationship was anymore, or what his feelings were toward her.

She took a few deep breaths in the hope of calming her nerves, but it only made her feel slightly dizzy. Running her hand along the wall to steady herself, she walked the few steps to his open door and stopped. She heard a voice inside, a feminine voice. She leaned forward just far enough to glimpse the back of a young woman who was standing in the room. She appeared to be a student, dressed in tight jeans and a pink sweater, and holding a notebook. Rather short of stature, the girl had long, very pale blond hair, whose loosely curled ends were left free to tumble over her shoulders. Stacie stepped back quickly and stood by the door frame, not sure if she should wait or interrupt them. She decided to wait.

"How long is it going to take you to grade the finals?" she heard the student asking in a tone that had no trace of shyness.

"A few days." It was Gray's voice; the voice she hadn't heard in so long. Low and soft with a distinctive edge, it had always had an effect on her. Her throat constricted. She put her hand to her lips to stifle her urge to cry. Through sheer will she stiffened and strengthened herself. She had to be stronger than this.

"Could you do my test first?" the high voice in his office was saying. There was an impertinent playfulness in the girl's tone.

"I do them in the order I find them," Gray said patiently.

"Need some help?"

"No!" There was a light laugh in his voice as he refused, as if he found the young woman's persistence entertaining.

"You're not very nice!" she chided him in a teasing way.

"That test was horrible! I may die of anxiety waiting to know if I passed."

"With your grade average you don't know how to fail a test. And whatever you may die of, I'm sure it won't be anxiety."

"You're heartless, Gray!"

Gray! Stacie's ears were pricked. Since when do his students call him by his first name? She had been listening with some interest, not so much in the conversation but in the cockiness of the girl's manner. Stacie would never have dreamed of speaking to any of her professors in such a way. What bothered her more was that Gray didn't seem to mind it. To the contrary he sounded amused.

"Will you be working on any digs this summer? Snaketown?" the blonde asked.

"Yes. I'll have one class to teach, but I want to do some field work, too. It may be Snaketown unless something else develops."

"Will you have any students working with you?"

"It's possible, but I usually take graduate students," Gray told her.

"I'll be a senior next year. Isn't that good enough?"

"I could make an exception. I'm afraid you'd be a disruptive force in the field though."

"Why?" she asked with astonishment.

"Most of my grad students are men, Angelica. You'd be too much of a distraction."

Angelica laughed heartily. "Well, that's not my fault. It's their problem!"

"That's one way of looking at it."

"Can I go on one of your digs then?"

"We'll see."

Angelica sighed, apparently disappointed at not getting a firm answer. "Will you be in tomorrow?"

"Yes."

"Good. I'll come by to see if you've graded my test yet. Bye!"

Suddenly the young woman stepped out the door, gave Stacie a glance, smiled, then moved on down the hall. Stacie stared after

54

her, noting the girl's gracefully provocative walk and bouncing curls. She had to admire the confidence the young student exuded, but concluded it wouldn't be difficult to acquire such an air when one had such stunning good looks.

Her face was flawless with large blue eyes and perfectly formed features. Stacie had noticed there was no hint of vulnerability in her countenance; in fact there was a ready flirtatiousness lurking about the eyes and mouth. Added to this was a well-developed bosom, shown to calculated advantage by her form-fitting sweater. The girl's hips were perhaps not as slim as they might be, but Stacie doubted many men would quibble about it. Taken as a whole, she was a knockout.

Dr. Wilmott had mentioned that Gray still attracted college girls who followed him about, Stacie reminded herself. Somehow she hadn't pictured them as looking and behaving quite like this one. She wondered if the department chairman was deluding himself in thinking that Gray was pining away for his estranged wife. With girls like Angelica throwing themselves at him, why should he?

Stacie leaned her shoulder against the wall for a moment. She now found herself in a somewhat more prickly mood than when she had first approached Gray's door. It wasn't enough to overcome her bad case of nerves however. But, knowing that she couldn't stay out in the hall forever, she straightened up and steeled herself as best she could. She stepped into the open doorway.

The small office hadn't changed. She saw Gray in profile, half-sitting, half-leaning against the edge of his desk, his tall manly frame relaxed in a careless pose. His head was turned away from her and he was looking out the window in the contemplative attitude Stacie had known so well.

She couldn't see his face, only the rise of his high cheekbone and his thick brown hair, which brushed his collar and the top of his ear. Growing weak in the stomach and knees, she felt herself captured, as she had been years ago, by his brooding, self-contained air.

How often in the past had she stared at him like this, without his knowing it? She had loved to study him in his pensive moods, trying to decipher his quietness and the hidden sensuality she could always feel beneath his calm surface. To see him there exactly as she remembered, only three-dimensional and real and not a shadowed memory, was like sustaining a physical shock.

She stood at the door, recovering, wondering what to do. Should she call his name? Walk up to him? Wait until he turned around? Too nervous to prolong this tentative situation, she curled her cold fingers into a fist and knocked lightly on the open door beside her. She stood frozen as she watched him turn around.

"Yes?" he said as he first glimpsed her. He stared at her intently for a moment, his tanned angular face calm and questioning.

Stacie's eyes warmed as she saw again the handsome countenance she had once adored. His name came to her lips, but her voice was barely a whisper as she pronounced it.

Gray's expression was quickly changing. He had become very still and the color was fading from his face. His brown eyes were wide and darkening from the blackness of their dilating pupils, making a contrast to his suddenly ashen features.

Concerned that he looked so shaken, she quickly went to him. She couldn't remember his ever appearing so shocked. "I'm sorry, I should have told you," she said when she reached him. "I thought . . ." She was going to explain that she had expected Dr. Wilmott to have informed him of her coming, but thought better of it.

She was standing in front of him now, looking into his unblinking eyes. His gaze was taking in every feature of her face. Was he convincing himself that it was really her? She wasn't sure, for his eyes had a curious aspect unfamiliar to her. Her heart was pounding at being so near to him again and under his close scrutiny. What was he thinking?

"Are you okay?" she asked gently. She touched his arm, but

56

when she felt the firmness of his muscled forearm beneath his shirt sleeve, she drew her hand away, trembling.

He seemed to come to his senses then and recoiled from her a bit, gripping the edge of the desk, hands on either side of his hips.

His color was more normal now, but his eyes still held traces of astonishment as he studied her. He seemed particularly preoccupied with the worry showing in her eyes, already shadowed and strained from nerves and lack of sleep.

His eyes took on an aspect of concern, even a sheen, and he drew his brows together slightly. Stacie was puzzled at his expression. If she was not mistaken, he was looking at her with something that resembled sympathy.

"Are you all right?" he asked softly. "Have you lost your job? Do you need money?"

Stacie was dumbfounded. He thought she had come back looking for his help? She felt rather insulted.

"My job sent me here. My editor wants me to interview you for an article in *American Traveler*. Maybe you didn't know— I'm one of their staff photographers now."

It occurred to her that he might think she was still freelancing.

His expression changed and the concern disappeared. "I know. I saw your name—your maiden name—listed in the magazine. Sorry. I thought something may have gone wrong with your position there."

"Not at all. They just promoted me to the status of writer too," she said with pride.

"I *see*. My mistake," he said in a pointedly apologetic tone. "And you've come to interview me?"

She smiled hesitantly, not sure of his attitude. "Yes. My editor saw the article about Snaketown in the *National Geographic*. He was intrigued with your ideas about ancient migrations from Mexico."

She paused to allow him to comment, but he said nothing.

57 .

Anxious and not knowing what else to do, she elaborated, her words coming out in a nervous rush.

"I'm supposed to explain your theory and get some good pictures. I'll need to find a dig other than Snaketown though. It's too flat and uninteresting. I was hoping you could suggest some more photogenic place that would support your theory."

As she spoke to him he was regarding her intently, but she felt his mind was not really taking in what she was telling him.

He stared at her in silence for a long moment. When he spoke his voice was laced with resentment.

"Two and a half years without a word from you, except for that postcard with your address on it. . . . Now when you do show up, it's to interview me for your damn magazine!"

She was surprised by his sudden hostility. "You expected me to write?" she asked incredulously.

"You were the one who left. You could have let me know how you were doing."

"I left because *you* wanted a divorce!" she said.

"It didn't mean I didn't care what happened to you!"

Stacie was appalled. "You could have fooled me! Why didn't you write to me, then? All you did was send my clothes."

"I figured you'd be too busy with your career to answer!" he said cuttingly.

"Obviously we've been misunderstanding each other's good intentions," she said. Her tone was anything but conciliatory. What nerve, she thought, looking upon himself as the injured party! He had destroyed their marriage and now was making her out to be the insensitive one. She couldn't resist returning his remark in kind. "What did you want, a pen pal?"

"No. I wanted a wife," he said with a martyred dignity that rubbed salt into her wounds.

"You asked for the divorce, I didn't! And while we're on the subject, why is it we're still married? My lawyer flew all the way out here. . . ."

"I believe," he interrupted her with a steady voice, "my attorney told your fancy New York lawyer that I had been too busy

58

to get all the papers he wanted. I'm an archaeologist and a university professor. I have neither the time nor the inclination to get involved in legal hassles. . . ."

"Your lawyer didn't even show up in court!" She said the words with as much force as she could, but he kept on talking as if she had not spoken at all.

"I have more interesting things to concern myself with than settling property and all that rigmarole."

"You don't need to worry about property," she said. "I don't want anything from you. I can support myself."

"So I see." There was a sense of angry resignation in his tone. He lowered his head slightly and glanced off to the side.

A silence fell between them for a few moments. Stacie decided she'd better concentrate on her magazine assignment for now, since their arguing wasn't accomplishing anything. She had to remember to put her job first.

"So . . . when do you think I can talk with you about the article?" she asked, taking care to calm her tone of voice.

Her words drew his eyes to her face again. He was silent for a short while, but she could tell by the intensity of his gaze that his mind was working.

"How is it that your editor is so interested in my theory?" There was an element of suspicion in his voice.

She shrugged. "He read about it in the *Geographic* and thought it was the sort of thing that would appeal to our readers." All at once it came to her what he might be thinking. "He didn't know we were married."

"He didn't?"

"Of course not! If you think I arranged this somehow . . ."

"I'm just asking a question."

"Look, I didn't even want to take this assignment, but it's the first one they're letting me write, and I didn't want to blow the chance. No one on the staff at *American Traveler* knows I was married. I made it a point never to discuss my personal life."

"How commendable! It left you looking so conveniently unattached. I see you've even discarded your ring, besides using your maiden name."

This was too much. She wanted to avoid arguing with him, but she couldn't let this pass by. "When I started my job, I thought I was being divorced. Why introduce myself as Mrs. Pierce and then have to explain a short time later that I wasn't Mrs. Pierce anymore? Using my maiden name and not wearing my ring was a way of keeping my personal life private. Why do you still wear yours? For honorable reasons, or because you want to protect yourself from predatory co-eds like that blonde who just strutted out of here?" She pointed to the open door for emphasis.

A light suddenly glimmered in his eyes, and Stacie instantly knew she shouldn't have mentioned the blonde. Gray was obviously assuming she was jealous, and it left her feeling peculiarly defenseless.

"I don't need protection from her, Stacie," he said smoothly.

Stacie lowered her eyes from his smug gaze. He had certainly won that round. Perhaps not. She decided to try again. "Then why *do* you wear your ring?" she asked, glancing down at the softly shining gold band on his left hand.

"We're still married. It never occurred to me to take it off."

What a nice, pat answer! She felt like strangling him. "Our marriage is a legal technicality! I don't know why you've let things drag out this way!"

"Is there some reason you're so anxious to get a divorce?" While his voice was calm, the impersonal tone he was using seemed a trifle forced.

"I simply want to have things settled! I'd like to be either married or single, not half in between. You were the one . . ."

"Which would you prefer to be, married or single?"

"What?"

"It's a simple question."

She stared at him in confusion, her breathing growing shallow.

"Surely you have some answer," he prodded.

"Married," she said, barely able to say the word.

"Well, you are married. Why worry about a divorce?"

Her face reddened and she was furious. "Why are you being so obtuse about this? We don't have a marriage and you know it!"

She could see ire rising in him. "Is that all my fault?"

She wanted to answer with a resounding *yes!* but held her tongue. Pressing her lips together she consciously reined in her anger. Above all else, she had to remain on speaking terms with him if she was to get her assignment done. "Gray . . ." Her voice was purposely soft and restrained. She noticed he looked away when she said his name. "I didn't come here to argue with you. I'm just here to do my article. We can settle our personal problems some other time."

"They're your problems not mine. A divorce won't solve anything for me."

"Okay," she said. Trying to be agreeable, she refrained from pointing out once again that the divorce had been his idea. "Now, about my assignment . . ."

"Yes, of course, your article!" he said with mocking enthusiasm. "How can I be of assistance?"

"Well, first of all I want to know if there's some dig besides Snaketown we could use?" She waited a few moments for his answer, but soon saw she wasn't going to get any. He was eyeing the soft mass of curls that framed her face.

"You don't like my hair," she said for him.

"*Is* that your hair?"

She sighed with annoyance. "Yes! I got a permanent."

"I thought maybe you stuck your finger in an electric socket."

She didn't want to let his remark wound her, but it did. "I'm sorry if I'm not your long-haired little Barbie doll anymore," she shot back.

"Doll? You used to be a human being. Now you're a cool, calculating robot."

"That's a horrible thing to say to anyone!" she said in a voice hushed with anger.

"Well, well! I'm glad to see you two communicating so nicely," a dry voice said from the doorway.

Both Stacie and Gray turned to glare at Dr. Wilmott.

"Sorry, but I couldn't resist." He took a step into the room. "I didn't mean to interrupt, but I have to remind Gray that we're going to Martin Caldwell's ranch this evening."

"I hadn't forgotten," Gray said. He stood up for a moment, but then leaned against the desk again. "You . . . remember Stacie. . . ." He raised his hand hesitantly toward his wife.

"Oh, we had a nice little reunion over lunch today," Dr. Wilmott said pleasantly. "She called me a few days ago to say she was coming out to do her article."

"Did she!" Gray turned an accusing gaze on Stacie. "How thoughtful of her."

Stacie turned away and walked to the window.

"Shall we go in my car?" Dr. Wilmott asked Gray.

Gray took his eyes off of his wife and looked blankly at the older man. "Go where?"

"To the Caldwell ranch."

"Oh. Sure."

"We can drop Stacie off at my home first, so she can borrow my daughter's car."

"Oh, no, Dr. Wilmott . . ." Stacie began to object, but was interrupted by her husband.

"Why use your daughter's? Stacie's got her own car sitting at home in my garage."

Stacie's eyes grew sharp and wide. "You still have it?"

"Well, maybe that's a better idea," Dr. Wilmott said with barely concealed enthusiasm.

"How do we know it still works? After all this time the battery's probably dead."

"It runs fine. I've kept it in good shape," Gray told her irritably.

"That's settled then!" Dr. Wilmott said before Stacie could

object. She was growing annoyed with his eagerness to push them together and gave him a warning look. Dr. Wilmott chose to ignore it.

"Let's see," he continued, "we're supposed to be at Caldwell's at seven thirty. It'll take at least an hour to get there. Why don't the three of us have dinner about five, then we can drop Stacie off. . . ."

What fun! Stacie was thinking. She didn't feel she could stomach a dinner with Gray's acid remarks and Dr. Wilmott's attempts to reconcile them, but she needed time to find a graceful way out of it. "Who's this Martin Caldwell you're going to see?" she asked with suddenly acquired interest before Dr. Wilmott could settle his plans.

"He recently inherited a large ranch up around Wickenburg. There's a ruin on his property that our university has been trying to investigate for the past thirty years. We've been to see him before and we're hoping to convince him tonight to let us at least have a look at it," Dr. Wilmott explained.

"It's not going to be easy," Gray muttered. He had picked up a Styrofoam cup of coffee from his desk and was watching the liquid swish as he moved his hand in a circular motion.

"What's the ruin like?" Stacie asked. She was growing more interested than she thought she would be.

"All we know is from some records made around nineteen hundred, but apparently it's a small cliff dwelling," Dr. Wilmott said. "It's located in a shallow cave in a hidden canyon. Not many people have seen it since it's not easy to find and the Caldwells were always tough on trespassers."

"It may not have been looted by pothunters, then," Stacie said, thinking aloud.

"Rumor has it that it's in pretty good shape. It might be an interesting one for your article," Dr. Wilmott suggested.

Gray raised his head and looked at Dr. Wilmott, alarm in his eyes.

"That's what I was thinking," Stacie said. "It sounds like it

63

may be picturesque. Do you think it might show evidence to support Gray's theory?"

"Now just a minute!" Gray said, putting down the cup so suddenly that the coffee splashed. "The main reason the Caldwells have refused to allow the ruin to be excavated is that they were afraid it would draw sightseers and reporters. The last thing he's going to want is to have a photographer from a well-known magazine taking pictures."

"Well, maybe I could come with you tonight and see what he says. It wouldn't hurt to ask," Stacie said.

"Of course it would!" Gray said severely. "Just your presence with us would make him question our motives. We've tried to assure him that his ranch wouldn't be turned into a tourist stop."

Dr. Wilmott was thoughtfully stroking his chin. "Martin Caldwell's a reasonable sort, not like his father was. I don't think Stacie's coming along can hurt."

Gray looked at Dr. Wilmott as if the older man had lost his mind. "Larry, six months ago he was still negative about the idea. I've had a hard time getting him to agree to even discuss it again. I think he only invited us over tonight to be polite. Bringing a magazine reporter with us is the worst thing we could do!"

"Oh, I don't know." Dr. Wilmott leaned against the doorway. "Maybe an attractive young woman can make more headway with him than we've been able to."

CHAPTER FIVE

Dinner did not go well. As Stacie had foreseen, the atmosphere was edgy in spite of Dr. Wilmott's amiable conversation. They were eating in a small restaurant near the university, a place popular with students. It was a new establishment since Stacie's time at school, but the college ambiance brought back memories of her undergraduate days.

As she sat with the two professors she realized, in a small moment of clarity over her chicken soup, that she no longer felt like a student with them, but as an adult and their equal. Like them, she was a professional with work experience of her own.

The realization came as something of a surprise. In former days she had felt intellectually intimidated and shy about taking part in their conversations, even though Dr. Wilmott had always encouraged her by his look and tone. Gray, after their marriage, had seemed pleased with her and clearly enjoyed her presence on any occasion, but had apparently been content for her to remain quiet and shy around his colleagues. She had accepted this as natural. She had only turned twenty-two and was twelve years younger than her husband. How could she have expected to converse on his level? She had felt honored that Gray wanted her with him at all.

What a difference two and a half years in New York had made. Now she could see it all so clearly: Gray had wanted her precisely because she was quiet and shy and so willing to follow his lead.

As she kept pace with Dr. Wilmott's talk of his daughter's studies abroad, she constantly kept Gray in view from the corner of her eye. He was silent for the most part, going at his dinner plate as though eating were an onerous task. She noted that she had somehow forgotten he was left-handed. It had been a curious thing to her when she first saw him, she remembered, watching him write on the blackboard in what seemed to her a backward sort of way. She recalled that after their marriage, she would clear their dinner dishes off the table and always find the handle of his coffee cup turned in the wrong direction.

His cup was turned that way now. She watched him reach across his plate to pick it up. When he brought it to his mouth he looked over the rim at her and saw her eyes focused on him. As he put the cup down again, a look of irritation hardened his brow. Stacie lowered her eyes to her plate.

"You must travel a lot with your job, Stacie," Dr. Wilmott said with interest, all at once placing the burden of conversation on her.

"Yes, I do," she said evenly, trying to collect herself. "I've been sent all over the country in fact. I think I have six states to go before I've been in every one."

"Do you enjoy it?" the older man asked.

Stacie saw Gray's eyes shifting from Dr. Wilmott to her, a cynical hardness in them. "Well, I love the photography itself, but I do get tired of planes and living out of a suitcase," she admitted.

"You mean there are drawbacks to being a career girl?" Gray taunted her in a falsely benign tone.

Her eyes went to his in a flash, and she stared at him. "Woman," she said. "Career *woman*."

Hostility entered his gaze. "Pardon me," he said with mock humility.

66

"Of course," she said with sharp politeness, carefully placing her napkin on the table. She had decided she was finished.

Gray did the same with his napkin, only he threw it down in a small motion of disgust. Dr. Wilmott watched them both and apparently thought it wise to follow suit. "Shall we go on to the ranch?" he said as though they were all in store for a treat.

They left the restaurant and piled into the front seat of Dr. Wilmott's car, Stacie in the middle. She did not like the arrangement and would have been happy to sit in the backseat. But Dr. Wilmott had conveniently placed stacks of books and term papers in the back, and she was reluctant to ask if they couldn't be moved to the trunk.

So as not to interfere with Dr. Wilmott's driving, she put both legs to the right of the hump on the floor and found her thigh often coming against Gray's. It was unnerving. His large, lean body so near to hers, touching her, brought back old sensations she would have been very grateful not to remember at that moment. She felt her senses heightening and her muscles tensing. It was a long drive; she had to get out of this riveting sensual surge his nearness was causing. She didn't want to want him that way. And he musn't know he could still arouse this reaction from her—he musn't even hope for it. He didn't deserve that satisfaction.

"Perhaps this would be a good time to get some of my interviewing out of the way," she said, forcing a smile.

"Good idea!" Dr. Wilmott said. Gray took a long breath and looked out his side window.

She addressed herself to her pointedly disinterested husband. "Could the Indians who you think migrated into Arizona from ancient Mexico have been Aztecs or Mayas? And did you find any proof for your theory at Snaketown?"

"No." Gray's tone indicated he was doing his best to be patient. "We don't find proof; we only find evidence that supports the theory."

"All right. Then what does the evidence suggest? Who were these people and what area do you think they came from?"

"Who were what people?" Gray asked.

"The . . . the ones who built Snaketown." Damn! She should have known better than to start this interview cold. Not wanting to think about Gray had made her avoid the review work she should have done. She had told herself she knew enough already, having taken Gray's class in southwestern archaeology. It was painful to recall now that she had spent more time thinking about him than the subject he was teaching.

"And what do we call that cultural group?" he asked as though prodding a small child to recite the ABC's.

"Anasazi," she said. The name sprang into her head from a hazy confusion of once-learned archaeological names and terms.

"And I gave you a B in my class!" Gray said, dismally shaking his head. "You must have crammed for the final and forgotten everything you learned the next day!"

Yes, that was exactly what she had done. Meeting him for their afternoon love sessions had taken a lot of her time, but she supposed he wouldn't think of that. "Anasazi wasn't right?" she asked. Her hands were growing fidgety and she was starting to feel like a student again.

Gray let out a sharp disgusted sigh. "You're supposed to write an article for a national magazine on southwestern prehistory, and you don't even know who built Snaketown?"

"Now, Gray," Dr. Wilmott interrupted, "Stacie's had a long day. She just flew in from New York and she's got a time change to adjust to. To her it's late in the evening already and she's probably tired."

"A career *woman* ought to be used to such things," Gray muttered.

"No, Gray's right. I should have reviewed this more. I . . . didn't have time," Stacie said. She turned and looked at Gray, anger flickering in her eyes. "Do you think you might take a minute or two to go over the facts and set me straight?"

"Oh, I'd love to set you straight!" he testily retorted.

Stacie faced forward again and glared out the front window, too angry to say a thing.

Dr. Wilmott calmly came to her rescue. "Stacie, it was the Hohokam who built Snaketown."

"Oh," she said, feeling stupid. Now it all came back in an instant. "Of course. The Hohokam were in the southern part of Arizona; the Anasazi were to the north. And there were a few smaller groups around, too . . . like the Salado Indians. Right?"

"There! You remember," Dr. Wilmott said with approval.

"What were the cultural differences between the Anasazi and the Hohokam?" Gray asked.

Snatches of class notes she had once drummed into her head came to mind. Hesitantly she said, "Their pottery was different. The Anasazi built multi-storied pueblos and buried their dead. The Hohokam lived in pit houses and cremated their dead . . . and they also built a very elaborate irrigation system."

"Well, there's hope!" Gray said sarcastically. "Now: Snaketown was the center of the Hohokam culture. What were the centers of Anasazi culture?"

"What is this, a surprise quiz?" Stacie said with annoyance.

"Yes. I want to know if it's worth my time giving you an interview."

"Mesa Verde and . . . and Chaco Canyon," Stacie answered grudgingly.

"And?"

"And what?" she snapped.

"The Anasazi had three centers of population," Gray reminded her.

Stacie's mind was a blank. "I don't remember the other one."

"No, of course not," he said softly, that martyred edge in his voice again.

His injured tone made her turn and look at him. "Well, what was it?"

"The Kayenta region." He turned to look at her. "Remember the Betatakin ruin?"

Betatakin. The name instantly flooded her mind with vivid images of a silent, abandoned city of red sandstone nestled in a huge, half-dome cavern in the high wall of a canyon. Shortly after she had graduated, Gray had taken her there. Because of his professional status, he had received permission from the park ranger at Navajo National Monument, where the ruin is located, to camp there overnight. Late in the day they had hiked down the steep trail to the bottom of the canyon and up the other side to the large ruin, sheltered by the awesome, high ceiling of the spacious cavern. The last rays of the sun were coming through the huge, round entrance.

She and Gray, like two actors on some long abandoned stage setting, watched the darkness fall over them like a curtain. Then the squared rooms and towers of the ruin became defined by ghostly moonlight. The total silence of the remote place seeped into them until Stacie began to wonder if she had become a spirit, like those she imagined were all about her in the cold, lonely, ancient city.

It was then that Gray had moved to put his arms around her. She had absorbed his warmth and felt his strength and knew she was alive. Inevitably, they made love. Their soft murmurs of passion whispered through the still ruin, but if any spirits were disturbed, Gray and Stacie were not aware of it. They awoke in each other's arms in their double sleeping bag the next morning, warm and content as the sunlight gradually invaded the cavern and a new day began.

Her eyes widened and grew lonely as Gray's eyes held hers. His gaze was both accusing and sad. They had forgotten Dr. Wilmott and the car speeding through the darkness down the highway. It was a suspended moment, a remembrance of shared happiness that was now a heartbreaking reminder of what they both had lost.

The muscles in Gray's jaw tightened. He turned and looked out the windshield again, his profile stony. Stacie faced forward also, suddenly aware of Dr. Wilmott's presence. Cold reality set in. The past couldn't be brought back again; it could only remain a spiritlike memory.

Dr. Wilmott, perhaps sensing the tension between them, broke the silence. "Stacie seems to remember her southwestern prehistory pretty well, Gray. Why don't you continue with the interview?"

Neither said anything for a few moments. At last Stacie said in a constrained voice, "Yes, I suppose we should." She took another moment to recall what the interview was about. "What supports your theory that the Hohokam migrated from Mexico?" She asked this of Gray, but did not turn to look at him.

His answer was slow in coming and his voice was flat. "There are many evidences," he began on a sigh. "The Hohokam had ball courts similar to those found in ruins in Mexico, platform mounds similar to the substructures of Mexican pyramids, the knowledge of irrigation—"

"Oh, wait," Stacie interrupted him and hurriedly began to unzip her large shoulderbag which was resting on her lap. "Let me get this on tape." She pulled out a small, battery operated tape recorder and pressed its play and record buttons. A soft whir told her the machine was functioning. "Okay. Ball courts, platform mounds, irrigation," she repeated for the benefit of her tape. "Go on," she said to Gray, glancing up at him.

He was looking at the tape recorder, then allowed his gaze to meet her eyes briefly. He regarded her as if she had suddenly become a stranger, someone he had just met and from whom he did not know quite what to expect.

She supposed it was odd to be talking to a person and have them suddenly pull out a tape recorder. But he ought to have anticipated some such thing from a magazine reporter. "Go on," she prompted him again.

"The . . . their pottery designs and animistic clay figurines resemble those found in Mesoamerica. They imported copper bells, pyrite mosaic mirrors, even parrots from Mexico. It's recently been speculated that the Casa Grande ruin was an astronomical observatory used to determine the equinoxes and solstices, similar to ancient observatories found throughout Mesoamerica. The ties with Mexico are very strong and, it seems to me, obvious."

"What do those who disagree with you think?" Stacie asked.

71

"Some archaeologists admit to a Mexican influence which came about by diffusion or trade, but they believe these changes were adopted by a people already living in Arizona. They can provide some good arguments for their viewpoint too. But I think the changes happened too suddenly to have come about only through a neighboring cultural influence. To me it's logical to think that a new group moved up from the more advanced civilizations to the south and brought with them the knowledge of irrigation, new technical skills, and new pottery designs. And not only did they come from Mexico, but I believe the Hohokam maintained their ties with the southern civilizations and functioned as the northern outpost of ancient Mexican culture."

"Really?" Stacie said, pleased with the information he was giving her, for it was exactly the type of thing Ben Hackett was looking for. She couldn't help but be impressed with Gray. He was as she remembered him when she first saw him in the classroom, his mind steeped in his subject and in full command of it. "How did they maintain the ties?"

"Mainly through a very active trading system," he replied, engrossed now in the conversation. "The Hohokam mined turquoise, which was highly prized by the Aztecs. They traded it for the copper bells, mirrors, ocean shells and birds from Mexico. The Hohokam also exported the cotton they grew, their turquoise, and some of the goods obtained from Mexico to the Anasazi in the north. I believe there's evidence of a long trade route established around the eighth century that allowed merchantmen to travel north from the Pacific Coast of southern Mexico, stopping at established trading centers all along the way, and ending at Snaketown, their northernmost outpost. Aztec trade merchants were also going far south into Guatemala for jade, and they traded with the Maya for cocoa and for rubber to make balls for their ceremonial games in the ball courts. One of these balls was found at Snaketown. And there's evidence that the Hohokam were worshipping the Mexican god Tezcatlipoca. So, you see, there are so many connections with Mexico, that it seems illogical not to think the Hohokam were an integral part of Mesoamerican civilization. But some of my colleagues will never be convinced until much more evidence is found. Archaeologists like to cling to their own pet notions."

"And that one is Gray's," Dr. Wilmott added wryly.

"Yes," Gray agreed with a little smile.

Stacie smiled too. She had always liked, and sometimes been amused by, Gray's tenacity. She used to joke that he could brood over broken potsherds and other bits of old rubbish for hours, tracing their significance. Her gentle ribbing would make him laugh at himself, but he never strayed from his preoccupation with his work. Unless, of course, a certain mood overtook them both. . . .

Stacie straightened in her seat and chastened her mind not to wander so easily. She had to think of her own work.

"This ruin at the Caldwell ranch, do you think it might reveal something to support your theory?" she asked.

"Probably not," Gray said.

Stacie was disappointed. "Why not?"

"Since it's a pueblo cliff dwelling, it probably wasn't Hohokam. More than likely, it was built by a stray Anasazi group. They weren't under direct Mexican influence, except through their contact with the Hohokam. It's an uninvestigated ruin and we want to find out what we can about it, but I'm not expecting to find anything there to support my claims."

"I see," Stacie said quietly and turned off her tape recorder. She had been hoping the ruin would be useful for her article. With a sigh she put the recorder back in her bag. She asked, "What's this Martin Caldwell like?"

"He's a pleasant enough fellow," Dr. Wilmott answered. "Doesn't seem to take after his ancestors. His father would slam the phone down on archaeologists who asked to see the ruin. And I hear his grandfather used to go after trespassers with a shotgun!"

Stacie chuckled. "Is he young? Old?"

"Oh, what would you say, Gray? About forty-five?"

Gray nodded in agreement.

"Does he have a large family?" Stacie asked.

"He's divorced, but he has people there who run the ranch for him. He's quite wealthy. His former wife is a faculty member, I understand. Did you say you've met her, Gray?"

"Once or twice," Gray replied. "She's in the Mathematics Department."

Dr. Wilmott had slowed the car's speed and appeared to be watching for a turn-off. It was growing dark, but Stacie could see that they were no longer on flat land, but in a more rolling terrain.

He turned onto another road and after a few miles came to a dirt road turnoff. A large, rustic arch made of wood was constructed over the road. The car's headlights barely illuminated the words at the top: THE CALDWELL RANCH. A small sign nailed to the bottom of the arch at car level was easy to read: TRESPASSERS WILL BE PROSECUTED TO THE FULLEST EXTENT OF THE LAW.

In spite of this silent admonition, Dr. Wilmott drove the car through the arch and continued slowly down a bumpy, narrow dirt road. After about a mile a few buildings came into view. As he approached the largest, Stacie could make out that it was modern in style with Spanish touches. She could see a tile roof and long veranda across the front.

Dr. Wilmott parked in front of the building and they all got out. She mounted the few steps up onto the tile-roofed porch. Large pots with small palms and desert plants were spaced along the veranda, interspersed with ornate wrought-iron chairs.

They approached a heavy wood double door and Dr. Wilmott rang the bell.

Stacie had half-expected to see some household employee answer, but quickly ascertained it was Martin Caldwell himself who opened the door. He greeted Dr. Wilmott and Gray in a polite, almost cordial manner, but Stacie felt a sense of intransigence in his bearing. She was a little surprised to find that he wasn't very tall, perhaps exceeding her height by only an inch or two. He had a broad shouldered, masculine build, somewhat barrel-chested, and a firm, but forbearing countenance. Stacie thought he was rather handsome. His features were regular and well-formed, and the gray that blended with his black hair above his ears gave his otherwise bland face a certain consequence.

They stepped inside onto a rich-looking, ceramic tile floor. He led them into a large room with a high-beamed ceiling, wood paneled walls, and a huge, stone fireplace which was presently not in use. The walls were covered with a number of original oil paintings of various sizes. They were mostly western landscapes, though there were a few colorful portraits of American Indians. The furniture looked comfortable, rustic, and expensive.

He had glanced at Stacie, no doubt wondering who she was and why she was there, but had said nothing. As he motioned for them to sit down, Dr. Wilmott said, "We've brought along a former student of ours. I didn't think you'd mind. This is—"

"Stacie Smythe," she said, preferring to introduce herself. She caught a glimpse of Gray's glowering eyes and turned her gaze back to Martin Caldwell. She was used to using her maiden name and saw no reason to take up her husband's again just because he was in the room.

"Happy to meet you," Caldwell said with a little smile.

Stacie took a seat next to Dr. Wilmott on a long, curved couch. Gray and Caldwell sat in matching easy chairs opposite each other, which with the couch formed a circular set around the fireplace.

"You ought to know, Mr. Caldwell," Stacie said in a straight-forward manner, "that I work for *American Traveler* magazine. I came back to Phoenix to do an article on prehistoric ruins in the area." She felt it was best to be above board with him from the beginning.

"Do you really?" he said with unexpected interest. A smile crossed his face again. "I buy that magazine now and then."

"Well, Stacie's one of their top photographers," Dr. Wilmott told him eagerly.

"No kidding. I've been interested in photography off and on. I'd like to talk to you a little about the equipment you use, if you don't mind. But we ought to attend first to Dr. Wilmott's and Dr. Pierce's reason for coming," he said, turning his head so that his gaze encompassed the two men. "I suppose you'd like me to consider some new proposition for exploring that ruin?" he asked them with tactful patience.

Gray remained silent, looking as though he were preoccupied with other thoughts. Dr. Wilmott took over. "No, nothing new to propose, Mr. Caldwell. We were hoping that you might have had a change of heart since the last time we talked to you. An uninvestigated ruin is like a missing piece of a puzzle. It could give us invaluable information. I appreciate your feelings on the matter but hope you recognize that withholding your permission to look over the ruin is a loss to science."

Caldwell courteously nodded his head. "Well stated, Dr. Wilmott. Please don't think I don't sympathize with your point of view. I don't know much about archaeology, but I respect your dedication. An old saying of my grandfather's was give an inch and lose a mile. I know if you see the ruin, you'll want to explore it, and pretty soon I'd have a full scale dig going on out there. And then we'd get amateur archaeologists and tourists who'd be asking to see it, and . . . and even magazine photographers like Miss Smythe here, pretty as she is." He said this with ironic humor and gestured toward Stacie. "I don't like to be the insensitive ogre who denies science it's right to pursue knowledge. But on the other hand I don't want my well-run ranch interrupted with all that commotion. But I've explained all this to you before; I'm afraid I haven't changed my mind."

Dr. Wilmott nodded his head and said lightly, "Well, we archaeologists are patient types. We never give up trying to turn over the last stone."

Gray leaned forward. He seemed to be concentrating on the discussion now, and his expression was serious. Unlike Caldwell and Dr. Wilmott, his tone contained no trace of humor. "If you like we could draw up a contract which stated what you would and would not allow us to do on your property. That would limit our investigation to your specifications."

Caldwell paused before replying but did not seem to give the suggestion serious consideration. "It's not a bad idea, but . . . no. I don't want to break a family tradition," he said with a smile, as though sensing it was a shallow excuse. He quickly changed the subject. "Look, there's some coffee going in the kitchen. Would you like a cup?" He glanced over the three faces, all a little blank with surprise.

Dr. Wilmott was the first to respond. "That would be nice. It's a long drive back."

Martin Caldwell was already out of his seat. "Have it ready in a jiffy."

When he was out of the room, Dr. Wilmott stretched back in the couch a bit and said, "Well, we're making some headway. This is the first time he's offered us coffee!"

Gray shook his head and mumbled, "We aren't getting anywhere with him."

In another minute Martin came back carrying a tray with four steaming mugs and cream and sugar crockery. Playing the good host, he passed them out one by one. When he got to Stacie he said, "It may be a little strong for you. Don't be afraid to use the cream."

She smiled at his thoughtfulness and poured in some extra from the creamer. "Thank you."

"So," he said as he took his chair again, "what kind of camera do you use, Miss Smythe? A four-by-five?"

"No. I've found large-format cameras too cumbersome," she answered, carefully holding the mug in her small hands. "I use only thirty-five-millimeter equipment. Is photography one of your hobbies then?"

"I suppose you could say that. Maybe I just like gadgets. I like to buy new equipment but I'm not too adept at using it."

"It takes practice," she said sympathetically. Before he could ask another question, as he appeared about to do, she said, "Pardon me for changing the subject, but this ruin on your property—do you see it often?"

He shook his head. "It's in kind of an out-of-the-way spot."

"I see," she said. "Have you or anyone else ever explored it or found artifacts there?"

A slow smile came over his face. "You *would* ask that," he said self-consciously. "The only time I saw the place close up was when I was about twelve. I rode over there on horseback one day and climbed up to explore it. In one of the rooms under some rubble I found an old pot or two and some broken stuff. Nothing much. But I did find a piece of pottery that looked sort of like a bird. I know an archaeologist would have disapproved of my removing it, but I did take it back with me. I was only a kid," he said rather apologetically.

She saw Gray's eyes sharpen and asked, "Do you still have it?"

"I do," he said, exhaling a sigh as if he'd known she was going to ask that. "You'd like to take a look at it, right?"

"If it's not too much trouble," she said, smiling at him sweetly.

Caldwell studied her bright eyes and expressive face for a moment, then chuckled as if at himself. "Of course not," he said in a quiet voice. "It's in another room. I'll get it."

When he was gone, Dr. Wilmott reached over and squeezed her wrist. "I had a hunch we should bring you along! Good work, Stacie!"

Stacie grinned at him conspiratorially. She was pleased with her little triumph too. When she cast her eyes over at Gray her smile faded. He looked as though he would like to get his hands around her neck.

She glanced away and her expression stiffened. Leaning forward, she put her coffee mug on the low table in front of her. *What was he so wrought-up about?* she was thinking. She'd have thought he would be eager to see the artifact.

Martin Caldwell came back into the room. Standing behind the couch, he leaned over Stacie and placed a heavy piece of pottery in her hands. It was rounded smoothly in the vague size and shape of a rather fat bird. Its head projected from a short neck and carried a prominent down-turned beak. Two large staring eyes were painted on each side of the head and the rest of the body had intricate designs covering the surface. It was

78

vividly painted in colors of red, black, and white. Even in modern times it made a striking art object. The thought occurred to her that it might be worth a great deal more than Caldwell seemed to imagine.

Forgetting herself in her excitement, she grasped the clay bird very carefully in both hands, got up from the couch, and carried it over to Gray. After safely putting it in his hands she kneeled down on the carpeted floor by his legs and watched him slowly turn the object about.

In doing this it didn't occur to her that she had reverted a bit to the former Stacie, the young girl who had hung on every word her professor said, who had unquestioningly run off and married him. If she had realized she was sitting at his feet again, both metaphorically and literally, she would have been angry with herself. But at the moment she only wanted to know what he was thinking and hear what he would say.

"Looks like a Salado polychrome," Dr. Wilmott said. He had moved to the end of the couch near Gray's chair and was leaning forward to get a better view. The thought that she may have slighted Dr. Wilmott by not giving *him* the figurine first had also never entered Stacie's mind. The head of the department, however, did not appear to be the least bit offended.

"Yes," Gray said very softly. There was a studiously restrained excitement in his brown eyes and his focus of attention on the object was such that he seemed to have become oblivious of everything else.

"What did you call it, Dr. Wilmott? Salado . . . something . . ." Caldwell asked. He was standing behind Dr. Wilmott now, watching them.

"Polychrome," Dr. Wilmott repeated. "It means multicolored. This particular color combination was used by the Salado Indians. Perhaps you've seen the cliff dwelling at Tonto National Monument in the Superstition Mountains?"

"Yes, I took my little daughter there a couple of years ago," the rancher answered. "She wanted to go there for some school project."

"That's a Salado ruin," Dr. Wilmott explained. "And the area around Tonto was the center of their culture. It's a little surprising to find evidence of the Salado over here, although the artifact could have been brought here by trade. We'd have to see more from your ruin to be sure exactly what group lived here." He turned from speaking to Caldwell and glanced back at Gray. After observing him a moment he said, "Well, what is it, Gray? I can see something's got you."

The direct question broke Gray's concentration. He handed the pottery piece to Dr. Wilmott and said, "Look at the markings along the sides and the front: Aztec. It must have been made locally, but I've never seen such a direct and perfect imitation of Aztec designs."

"Yes, it does look like it was copied from the real thing," Dr. Wilmott agreed. "Very unusual."

"Really?" Caldwell said, diligently studying the object over Dr. Wilmott's shoulder as if he were seeing it for the first time.

From her position on the floor Stacie looked up at Gray. "How could that have happened?" she asked, staring at him until he turned his face to her.

He was about to answer, but when he looked at her the words seemed to catch in his throat. Her green eyes were clear and wide and her attention solely on him, waiting for his reply. In an instant he seemed lost in her gaze. His eyes softened and grew luminous with something that greatly resembled adoration.

His look took her breath away and her stomach plummeted as if she were in an elevator that had suddenly begun to rise. Now his eyes were moving over her face and a faint smile deepened the lines in his cheeks, making him look devastatingly handsome. He leaned toward her. In a doting voice he said, as if speaking to a little girl, "That's what we'd like to find out."

She gave him a small trembling smile and then shyly looked down. Her hands were shaking. What she saw in his eyes was more than she could cope with. She was learning much too rapidly that he still had the ability to shatter her with a look. The revelation was both frightening and wonderful. And dangerous, her instinct was sharply warning her.

Still trembling, not daring to look at him again while she was so near to him, she got up from the floor and went back to sit on the couch. She took a breath and tried to compose herself.

Cautiously glancing up at Gray, she saw his brown eyes on her, lustrous with warmth and triumph. It was clear he had assumed from her reaction that he could win her back. Stacie could feel him thinking that she was his again.

Her gaze tremulously meeting his, her eyes silently said back to him, "Yes, I want to be yours! But you have to understand me. It can't be the same as before."

She wondered if he *could* understand her. She feared he was only seeing what he wanted to see—what in a weak, unthinking moment she had allowed him to see—that part of her that longed for him and wanted him more than anything. What she feared he would not recognize was the other part of her nature that needed to maintain its own identity and not become lost in his.

She knew now and was overjoyed that he still wanted her. But the possessive, nurturing warmth in his eyes told her that he hadn't yet begun to comprehend what she was all about. He wanted the clinging, childlike woman who had sat at his feet a few minutes ago waiting for him to speak.

Could he be made to understand that the child in her had been counterbalanced by her growth in other directions? It might reappear from time to time, but it would never again be her whole self.

She had to hope that he could comprehend and eventually accept this. She needed him in her life again, she realized, just as she needed her career. Lacking either, she was incomplete.

The warmth in Gray's eyes as he watched her was dimming gradually. She could see his confidence slipping and being reluctantly replaced with confusion. He had not quite seen the response he was looking for.

Poor Gray, she thought. He always seemed to think it should be so simple. Perhaps she had led him to believe it could be. She had, after all, run off to Las Vegas the moment he asked her to marry him. And now, in another moment, she had suddenly run to him again. Why shouldn't he conclude she was willing to take up where they had left off? She must be more careful from now on what unintentional messages she might be giving him. Above all, she must never sit at his feet again—in any sense of the words.

She pulled her eyes away from Gray's. Dr. Wilmott was still discussing the clay bird with Martin Caldwell, and she forced herself to ignore Gray's intent gaze and concentrate on what they were saying.

"You see," Dr. Wilmott was explaining, "Mexican influence in ancient local cultures was usually much more diluted. Designs would be copied and recopied and altered a bit each time as pots and clay pieces were traded and imitated from group to group. But this piece almost looks as though someone from the heart of the Aztec world had painted it. Only the polychrome colors indicate it must have been made here in Arizona. We really should take this to our laboratory to check it further, perhaps get some date on it. Do you think you might allow us to do that?"

Caldwell straightened up. He had been leaning forward on his arms on the back of the couch to study the object in the older professor's hands. He glanced at Stacie, whose eyes were lambent and troubled.

"Sure, go ahead," he told Dr. Wilmott. "I guess it's the least I can do," he added and shot a self-deprecating grin at Stacie. She hesitantly smiled back.

He took a step closer to her end of the couch. "What was your purpose in coming here, Miss Smythe?" He was still smiling and his voice was friendly. "Were you hoping to get some photographs of the ruin?"

"Yes." Her voice was weak. "Yes, I was," she repeated in stronger tones. "Part of my assignment is to get photos of some of the lesser known ruins in the Southwest. Yours would certainly qualify."

82

"You're right, it would be the first pictures of it ever published."

"Have you ever taken any photos there?" she asked him.

"As I've told the two professors here in the past, there are some somewhere, but I wouldn't know where to begin to find them. This home was built about eight years ago and the old ranch house was torn down. A lot of things got lost or moved around in the process."

"I see," she said, casting her eyes down and sounding disappointed.

Caldwell shifted his stance restlessly. "You see, if a photo was published in a magazine, it would just draw people here," he told her earnestly, ignoring the two other interested parties in the room.

"I could agree not to mention the location or your name—just call it an unexcavated Arizona ruin," she suggested.

Caldwell slowly grinned again. "You're pretty quick, aren't you? An answer for everything!"

Stacie laughed a little at his wry compliment. "That's part of my job, I guess," she said.

"I bet you're darn good at your job too," the rancher said.

"Yes, I am," she answered with a smile, deciding to let her self-confidence show since Caldwell seemed to admire it. She flitted a glance at Gray and saw dark thunderclouds in his eyes. Quickly she looked back at the rancher's frankly interested countenance. She wasn't about to let Gray ruin her composure again.

Caldwell's hazel eyes studied her a moment. He drew himself up and let out a long, calculated sigh. "You all must have caught me in a good mood today," he announced as though amused with himself. "I'll tell you what: I'll let the three of you look over the ruin." He turned toward the two professors. "You gentlemen can do some research there if it seems worthwhile to you. I'll even donate any artifacts you find to your university. I'll have my lawyer draw up appropriate papers. My stipulations are that only the two of you work there and that you keep it quiet. I don't

83

want it mentioned in the local papers and I don't want any big work parties coming out and doing a full-scale excavation. And I don't want any tractors or other big equipment on my land.

"And you, Miss Smythe," he said, turning now to Stacie, "may take as many pictures as you like. But I have two stipulations for you: one, that you don't mention the location in your article; and two, that you let me observe your photgraphic techniques while you're taking the pictures. How's that?"

Stacie laughed in surprise and her smile was radiant. "It's fine with me! Dr. Wilmott?"

Dr. Wilmott was equally pleased. "Sounds great! We'll be happy to comply with your wishes, Mr. Caldwell. As far as using heavy equipment, tractors and such would be totally unnecessary at this type of dig. Thank you for reconsidering," he said, extending his hand to shake Caldwell's. He turned in his seat. "What do you think, Gray?"

"Yes, it sounds fine," Gray said, his stilted enthusiasm sounding as though he were acting a part. Then he looked up at Caldwell and said in a low voice that was tainted with sarcasm, "Thank you."

Martin Caldwell was in too buoyant a mood and too taken with Stacie's smile to notice. Shortly afterward his three visitors left, after setting a time two days hence to see the ruin.

On the drive back to Phoenix, Gray said little. Stacie sensed his disgruntled mood, but wasn't sure of the reason for it. She stuck to safe ground by talking mostly to Dr. Wilmott. They speculated on the ruin and on the history of the clay bird Caldwell had allowed them to take with them. He had found a small box for it and they had put it safely on the floor of the backseat.

After listening to some of Dr. Wilmott's ideas Stacie decided to chance speaking to the brooding Gray. "Do you think that bird or other finds at the ruin may support your theory?" she asked.

"Probably. That should make you very happy," he muttered with ill-humor.

"What do you mean?"

"It will make such good copy for your article, won't it?" he said to her, eyes blazing.

Stacie was taken back by the scathing reply. She did not tempt his anger by saying anything more.

Dr. Wilmott dropped them off at the university parking lot near Gray's car. To Stacie's dismay he stuck to Gray's suggestion that she use her old car and did not repeat the offer of using his daughter's car. She wished he would have so she could have taken him up on it. She would have much preferred to be driving off with Dr. Wilmott than Gray. She knew she was in for more angry words or worse.

As Dr. Wilmott's car sped away Gray was opening the passenger door to his. He silently motioned for Stacie to get in, then walked around the other side and slid behind the wheel.

It was smaller than Dr. Wilmott's auto, a VW Rabbit with bucket seats in front and the gear shift in between.

"When did you buy this?" Stacie asked him hesitantly, testing the water.

"Last year." There was still hostility in his tone.

"Why didn't you use my car, since you've kept it in repair? It was newer than your old one and you wouldn't have had to buy this one," she questioned curiously.

"Because it's yours! I bought it for you," he said in a sharp, resentful voice. "Why the hell are we discussing cars?"

"Sorry!" she replied in kind. "Are you mad at me for some particular reason?"

He pulled the Rabbit out onto the street, then briefly glared at her in the darkness. "Shouldn't I be, *Miss Smythe*?"

"Stacie Smythe is my professional name. Why shouldn't I use it? I'm here on assignment," she said, genuine anger entering her tone of voice now. "I can't help it he assumed I was single."

"Why should he assume anything else, since you threw away your wedding ring!"

"I didn't throw it away!" she retorted. "I just stopped wearing it because you wanted to divorce me. Honestly, we keep going in circles with this argument!"

85

Gray stared ahead tensely and said nothing for a while. When he spoke again his voice was full of accusation. "You seemed to enjoy making eyes at Caldwell to get what you wanted."

"It was what you wanted too," she said defensively. "I wasn't making eyes. I was just being friendly." She thought this statement was accurate enough.

"Sure! And while you were at it, you flirted with me too. Just what were you hoping to get from me? Some exclusive discovery to put in your article? Or can't you resist flirting with men in general—even estranged husbands?"

Stacie's lips trembled just slightly as she sought for some answer. "I wasn't f-flirting with you. I just wanted to know what you thought of the clay bird."

"How can I have been so mistaken?" His voice was sardonic and mocking. "I could have sworn you were just like that doe-eyed co-ed who used to follow me around campus and look up at me in class with big innocent eyes."

"Oh, stop it!" she whispered harshly, feeling humiliated.

"You don't remember those days?"

"Of course I remember!"

He took his eyes off the road and stared at her. "Well, why did you look at me that way again? Do you like toying with me?"

"I wasn't . . . I don't know why I behaved that way. There's no reason for you to make anything of it. I'm not trying to recapture the past, if that's what you're thinking." There was no use trying to explain to him her state of mind. Her words would be wasted. He saw everything about their relationship in black and white. There was no room in his reasoning for shades of feeling.

He said nothing more. They were entering the neighborhood where Gray's house—and formerly hers—was located. In a few minutes they had turned into a driveway and pulled up next to a new Jeep. And there in front of her was the adobe, hacienda-style home with the pebble-covered front yard and cactus plants where she had lived so briefly. A wistful, sinking feeling came over her.

86

Gray got out of the car and came around to open her door. "Why don't you come in for a minute?" he said when she had stepped out of the car. There was a trace of unsteadiness in his voice.

"No, I . . . it's late. . . ."

"Only ten thirty. You might as well see the inside again too," he said, watching her look over the house.

She didn't reply and rather numbly allowed him to lead her to the front door. He pulled his keys out of his pocket and fingered through the large number of them attached to the leather holder. She recognized that the holder was one she had bought for him shortly after they were married. It had been a rather expensive one on sale, and Stacie couldn't resist getting it for him. As he fumbled with the keys under the porch light, suddenly a few came off and fell onto the welcome mat.

"This thing's always falling apart lately," he muttered as he bent to pick up the fallen keys.

"You should get a new one," she told him, her voice sounding a little hollow.

He said nothing as he turned the door key in the lock. They walked in and he switched on the lights.

The living room looked just as it had when she had left it: the dark wood beams crossing the ceiling, the rounded adobe fireplace projecting out from one corner of the room, the large bookcase covering one wall, and the Navajo rugs and Indian artifacts decorating the other walls. The low, heavy wood table still dominated the middle of the room, surrounded on three sides by a sofa and easy chairs.

It had all been Gray's original furniture. Stacie had done nothing to change it except to add a few potted plants, some of which were still there—and still alive. They looked overgrown and spindly. Gray probably never thought to fertilize them or cut them back. She was surprised that he had remembered to water them.

It had been in this room where they had had their last terrible argument. She had returned from that fateful assignment in

Alaska, hoping he had forgotten his threats to divorce her. But he hadn't. His words that night sped through her mind now:

"Our marriage isn't worth a nickel anymore," he had said harshly, an emptiness in his eyes. "You've already changed. You'll never be content with me after this. You want the world and I can't give you that."

"Gray," she had replied, "what are you saying? I love you!"

"Do you!" he had flung back with heavy irony. "So much that you have to have a career that takes you away from me all the time. And I'm supposed to be content in an empty house, wondering where you are! That's not good enough for me, Stacie. If you really loved me, it wouldn't be good enough for you either!"

"When you proposed," she had told him, "you said you knew I would grow up. Can't you let me do that? Do you expect me to be happy forever, locked away at home here, never accomplishing anything on my own?"

His jaws clenched. "Most wives are happy to live with their husbands. That's usually what they got married for. And most wives are willing to make compromises!"

"Are husbands exempt from making compromises?" she had responded with resentment. "Why is it me who has to make all the adjustments? Your life and career haven't changed a bit. Only now your house is vacuumed, dinner is on the table, and your bed has an added convenience. You wanted a plaything with no mind of her own. Not a wife!"

Oh, what terrible words and deep hurts had jarred the peacefulness of this room, this very same room where he had proposed to her and warned her to think carefully before marrying him. And the same room where in the quieter days of their marriage they had often sat together on the couch after dinner and made love.

Her chin was quivering now and her eyes glistening.

Gray was watching her. "What are *you* getting upset about?" he asked in a dry, taunting way. "*I* have to live here."

His tone set her back up. He always saw only himself as the

88

injured party. "Why didn't you change the furniture if you didn't want to be reminded?"

"I did, in the bedroom. Couldn't sleep. Would you like to see?"

"No!" Her voice was a hoarse whisper which came from the depths of her being. "I'd like to get my car and leave," she said, making her voice as strong and unyielding as she could.

He came close and stood in front of her. She could feel the heat from his body as he towered over her. "That might be difficult."

"Why?"

"My car and the Jeep are blocking the driveway to the garage. You can't move them without the keys—keys that you don't have."

"Are you saying . . ." She stopped speaking and gasped as she felt his arms closing around her torso, pulling her against him.

"I'm saying that you're welcome to spend the night here with me."

"No!" she cried, pushing against him with her hands.

He kept her tightly to him so that her struggles were useless. He bent his head toward her. She could feel his heart pounding. His breath flamed onto her cheek and his eyes, dark and urgent, were boring into hers.

"Stay with me, Stacie," he murmured. "Make love with me again. You must be plagued by memories of what we had together, like I am. The way you looked at me tonight . . . I know you want me. Show me!" He began kissing her throat, his lips heated and moist. "I've been aching to touch you all night. . . ."

He brought his mouth close to hers. His caresses had mesmerized her. She wanted to turn her face away but couldn't. His mouth fastened onto her parted lips with obstinate passion, as though he would never again release her. The breath was forced from her lungs and she became like a frail reed in his arms.

He pushed her head back and invaded her mouth with a deep, penetrating kiss. She quivered with the sudden incre͏ timacy, so clearly a reminder of what he ultimately w her. Unable to breathe, overtaken with his streng͏ ened by the paralyzing shock of her own reawakened needs, she felt herself growing lax.

His firm embrace kept her against him. He took his mouth away, then picked her up in his arms and carried her to the sofa. Sitting down beside her, he took her again in his arms but more gently this time. One hand curled around her small rib cage, just beneath her breast. His other hand was at the side of her neck, his thumb reaching up to keep her chin tilted toward his face while his gentle kisses rained over her face and mouth. Recovering, she began to answer them eagerly with her own, all the while longing for the hand by her midriff to reach up and caress her breast.

She wanted him with an intensity she had forgotten she could feel. It was like a physical pain, and she wanted to beg him to give her comfort as only he could.

Soon his hand rose to her small breast. She could feel the heat of his fingers through her thin blouse, seeking, enjoying her soft flesh. The warmth and pressure on her sensitive nipple sent a quivering sensual response through her body. An agonized gasp escaped her lips.

He responded by devouring those lips again, then whispering, "Oh, Stacie, I've missed you so much. I want you so much!"

Before he could go further, she pushed her hands against his shoulders. "No, Gray, please . . ." she begged, her voice choking with the deepening ache of desire. Tears came into her eyes. She was so torn by the warring emotions within her, she felt she would break into pieces.

"But you want me too! I can see you do!" he argued hoarsely.

"Oh, Gray," she cried helplessly, leaning her forehead against his shoulder and sobbing. He held her gently against him, his hands stroking her slender back in a comforting motion. But it gave her no comfort; it only made her want his caresses more, and she knew what deep sensual fulfillment could be hers if she only gave in to him. With all her resolve she determined she wouldn't give in. She musn't.

He rested his cheek against her curly dark hair. "There's no need to cry," he murmured soothingly. "It's not so terrible to want your husband, is it?" He spoke as though to a child.

She drew herself away and looked up at him. "But, Gray, we have so many problems," she said earnestly, through her tears. "It won't help to . . ."

"It might help us solve them," he softly suggested, looking at her with warm, urging eyes.

She shook her head, squeezing her eye lashes together so that tears fell. "I know we're ph-physically drawn to each other, b-but there has to be more than that. You have to understand my . . ."

He put a long finger to her lips, silencing her. "I understand that we want each other . . . that we always have from the very beginning. Even after two and a half years apart, it's still the same. All problems seem to fade beside that reality."

He leaned in to kiss her again. She put her hand to his cheek to prevent him. His skin was smooth and firm and warm in her palm, and he nestled sensually against her hand. She looked again at the manly face she had adored for so long and new tears streamed down her cheeks.

Her hand dropped from his face and she bowed her head. She was ashamed of herself. She couldn't stop her crying. She was behaving like the helpless child he wanted her to be. Her adult self seemed to have deserted her and she was at a loss as to what to do.

His gentle, warm fingers reached out to wipe away her tears. "Poor Stacie," she heard him say. "Don't cry. You're just upset and tired."

"Yes," she said, seizing on his sympathetic words. "I . . . I'm very tired. I really need to be alone for a while, Gray. I need time to think. Please let me have the car and I'll drive back to my place. I haven't even unpacked yet. Please, Gray . . ."

She hated the way she sounded, begging like a child. But at the moment it was the only way she could think of to handle him. She looked up at him with beseeching eyes.

His longing eyes seemed to melt in painful disappointment. His forehead creased and slowly he lowered his gaze from hers.

He couldn't hurt her if he tried, Stacie realized as she saw him about to acquiesce to her wishes. How could you not love a man who would never hurt you? She began to weep anew.

"Shh, Stacie. I'll let you have the car. Are you all right?" His fingertips moved over her cheek. "Maybe I should drive you to your place," he said with concern.

"No!" she said, straightening up and sniffing back her tears. She had to get away from him before she caved in to her own loving emotions. "No, I'm all right. But please, will you move your car so I can leave now?"

And he did. As she drove back alone to her condominium, the dull ache of unfulfilled need still weighing on her body, she had to marvel at it all. As long as she behaved like his little girl, she could wrap him around her finger. He would even put aside his own sexual passion at her tearful request.

But she was an adult now. She had to remember that. It was no good to allow herself to regress just because she wanted Gray back. She had come too far. Gray would have to learn that too—if he could.

CHAPTER SIX

The next day Stacie drove to the university to begin some research in the Archaeology Department's library room, located in the same building that the staff's offices were. She managed to put it off until early afternoon by using the morning to finish unpacking and to put her camera equipment in order.

The latter was unnecessary, since she was very careful about keeping her equipment clean and organized at all times. In truth she admitted to herself as she ate lunch alone in a small restaurant, she was hesitant about seeing Gray again. She didn't want to repeat her behavior of the previous night but wasn't sure what sort of attitude to replace it with. How could she keep her composure, comport herself like the mature woman she was, and yet not alienate a man who wanted her to be the child she once was?

She had been in the library room for a few hours looking through books and records Dr. Wilmott had suggested, when she found herself faced with the reality of that question. Working diligently at a long wood table, she was interrupted by the sound of footsteps. She looked up to find Gray standing near her chair.

"I was wondering if you were around somewhere. Why didn't

you come to see me?" he asked, looking down at her with slightly perplexed eyes.

"I . . . wasn't sure what your class schedule was," she answered.

He squatted down beside her, one knee on the floor, so that his eye level was nearer hers. "I don't have one anymore," he said with a smile that made her heart begin to melt. "I just gave my last exam for the semester. I'm through for a while."

"You must be glad."

"I am," he said. "I can spend more time with you." His tone was soft and meaningful, his eyes full of warmth. She saw the amber highlights that shone in their brown depths. "Stacie," he said, dropping his gaze and reaching out to put a hand over one of hers, "I'm sorry if I tried to move too fast last night. You're right. We have old problems that need to be squared away. We need to take our time with them and get to know each other again. I want to work them out—I need you back in my life."

The large palm of his hand was slowly rubbing the back of hers, causing the seed of desire to spring to life within her once more. She tried to smother it and keep her mind from wandering to unbidden memories of his caresses.

"Do you, Gray?" she said in a voice that sounded more vulnerable than she would have wished.

"Yes, Stacie," he said with hushed passion. "I would have shown you last night how much . . ." he paused as if catching himself, "but it was too soon, wasn't it? You need time to . . . to adjust."

Adjust? A warning signal flashed through her. He felt *she* needed to adjust? *If that was what he meant, he'd have to think that through again,* she told herself. She welcomed a sudden new sense of commitment to her own goals strengthening the will power that was going haywire under his touch.

He was watching her, apparently trying to read the subtle facial signs signaling that thoughts unknown to him were going through her mind. His hand squeezed over hers. "Why don't we have dinner together tonight?" he suggested quickly, as if to stop her mind from working. "We could go to that restaurant I took you to the first time we went out together."

"I'll have dinner with you. But not there," she said, her tone quiet and serious. "I think we should start fresh, don't you? Let's go to a place that doesn't have old memories connected with it."

His brown gaze seemed slightly mystified, but he said, "All right. How about . . . there's a new Italian place not far from our house. I've heard it's good."

She nodded in agreement, though something in her wished it wasn't near "our house."

"Were you planning to work here the rest of the afternoon?" he asked. She nodded again. "Good," he said. "I have some tests to grade. I'll come back here about five thirty and we can go then."

Stacie's mind was working quickly. "I think I'd want to change first, Gray. I don't want to wear blue jeans to a nice restaurant," she said, indicating her casual clothes. "Why don't you give me the address and I'll meet you there, say at six?"

It was a matter of logistics. She didn't want to be maneuvered into driving with him in his car again. If they left from the university, he would probably insist they go together instead of driving in separate cars. And when dinner was over, he might find some excuse for them to stop by his house again, a situation she wanted to avoid. It would be safest, she decided, if she drove her own car.

Gray chuckled. "The place isn't that fancy. People wear blue jeans almost anywhere nowadays. You look beautiful as you are!"

The compliment from his lips touched her inside, especially after his disparaging comments about her hair the day before. But she maintained her stand, feeling guilty that she was being tricky with him. She hoped there would come a day when she could be straightforward and not have to resort to feminine wiles to keep control over situations.

"Thank you, but . . . this is a special evening. I want to look especially nice." She managed to keep her gaze from wavering and looked straight in his eyes.

He drew his brows together. "But you'd have to go all the way back to your place."

"I don't mind."

"All right, look," he said, sighing, "give me your address and I'll come and pick you up."

She was growing edgy at his insistence and a new firmness entered her voice. "That's not necessary, Gray. I'll meet you at the restaurant." She smiled then, hoping it would soften her words.

He studied her steady gaze and a trace of suspicion entered his eyes. He had correctly realized there was more to this than her wanting to look pretty. "Are you worried I was going to try to sleep with you again? I promise there won't be a repeat of last night," he told her earnestly.

She nodded her head, accepting the sincerity of his word, but said, "I'll meet you at the restaurant, Gray."

The look in his eyes grew confused and wary. She had never used that quiet, firm tone of voice with him before. "All right," was all he said. He took his hand from hers. After giving her the restaurant's location he left.

That evening she met him and they had a quiet dinner. They spoke of many things: the dry spell in Arizona, staff changes at the university, a new class in Mesoamerican cultures Gray was considering, Dr. Wilmott's plans for retirement. Stacie tried to talk about her job and her travels, but noticed the subject was always imperceptably changed to something else.

For some reason the past and their remaining problems were avoided, even though Stacie had thought they were meeting together to begin work them out. Isn't that what Gray had said he wanted?

But she couldn't blame him entirely; she hadn't known how to begin working things out either. In some ways, through that dinner, they had talked to each other like strangers. When it was over he invited her to his house and she refused. He accepted the turndown without comment, no doubt expecting it. They went to their separate cars and drove off in different directions. Stacie came back to her condominium feeling empty and depressed.

The next morning she drove to the university, met Gray and Dr. Wilmott, and they went together in Gray's Jeep to the Caldwell Ranch. Martin was waiting and ready when they arrived. With no further ado he joined them, sitting in the back of the Jeep with Stacie. Following the rancher's directions, Gray drove them down a dusty, rutted dirt road for about a dozen miles. The terrain grew more and more rough as they went deeper into the foothills of the rugged Bradshaw Mountains.

Martin pointed out a dry gulley that crossed over the road, making a dip in it. He told Gray to turn off the road and they drove down the bone-dry stream bed. After several miles of bumpy, slow driving, the ground level on either side of them rising, they found themselves in a small canyon. There were a few leafy trees growing along the stream bed, hanging on until the next rain made the stream briefly flow again and flood their thirsty roots with water. The green trees made a refreshing change from the dry scrub vegetation and cacti which sparsely covered the landscape.

The stream bed made a turn. There ahead and above them in a hollowed out cave in the canyon wall was the ruin. It was quite small in comparison to Betatakin and the Mesa Verde ruins but picturesque and no less intriguing.

Made of buff-colored stone, it matched the canyon walls into which it was snugly built. The gently sloping roof of the cave sheltered it. It appeared to have several small, contiguous, one-room houses. On one end, reaching to meet the cave's roof, was a towerlike structure, it's walls half fallen away. At one time it was perhaps three rooms high, judging by the three windows or doors that interrupted its still intact side wall. Another structure near it appeared to have been two stories high.

They got out of the Jeep, Stacie taking along her carrying case of camera equipment. Martin fell in step beside her as the four of them approached the steep grade of dirt and rubble that had to be mounted in order to reach the ruin.

Dr. Wilmott and Gray, both wearing heavy climbing boots, began trodding up the slope in the dry, rocky dirt. Halfway up they stopped and both, as if of one mind, scooped up some soil. Sifting through his handful carefully, Gray came across what looked like a pebble. Stacie knew it was probably a potsherd. He handed it to Dr. Wilmott and bent to search for more.

"Find something?" Martin asked as he began to climb the slope himself.

"Pieces of broken pottery," Dr. Wilmott said, picking one off the ground himself. "You see, this was the trash dump for the people who lived here. It's typical of this type of ruin. If a pot broke, it got thrown down here along with the dinner scraps. Sometimes they buried their dead in the front slope too."

"Doesn't sound very sanitary," Caldwell remarked. He turned as Stacie was struggling up the steep grade to join them. She was wearing sturdy laced shoes and picking her way as carefully as she could, but was finding the going difficult. The heavy equipment bag slung over her shoulder did not help. Suddenly the eroding ground gave way under one foot. She found herself on her hands and knees as the shoulder bag slipped off and hit the ground.

"Here, let me help you," Caldwell said, instantly at her assistance. Taking her arm in a firm grasp to help her up, he said, "I'm sorry, I should have offered to take that case."

Stacie smiled her thanks, still struggling to regain an upright position in the loose rocky soil.

Gray, who had thrown the potsherds in his hand back onto the ground, stepped down toward her. "Here, give it to me," he said in an annoyed tone of voice. He extended his hand to take it.

Caldwell picked up the case and slung it over his own shoulder. "No, I can take it," he assured Gray in an easy tone.

Gray's eyes slid from Caldwell to Stacie, who was wiping the dust off herself. "Did you scrape your hands?" he asked her sharply. He took her hands in both of his and turned them over to inspect the palms. A scrape on the heal of one hand was bleeding slightly. "There's a canteen in the Jeep. You'd better wash that off," he said abrasively.

She didn't like his tone and pulled her hands away. "I'm all right."

"Why don't you be more careful! Haven't you got some better shoes to wear?"

"These are good shoes. I can't help it if I don't have big feet like you men!" she said curtly.

Caldwell laughed, and then Stacie found herself grinning at her own remark. She thought it was to the point. After all, heavy shoes like men wore would grab into the soil better.

Gray was not amused. He reached to take her arm. "Come on, I'll help you up," he ordered.

"I can get up there by myself!" she argued. She didn't like his attitude at all. He had hardly said anything all morning, preferring to reside in some enigmatic mood of his own. Now he was ordering her around. It wasn't her fault that Martin Caldwell had shown more thoughtfulness toward her than he had.

Gray was in no mind to argue. He put a strong arm around her back above her waist and pulled her along as he climbed the rest of the slope. She went along without further word, but she did not like his manner. When they reached the top he said, "The ground is uneven up here and there are a lot of rocks." He pointed to the fallen masonry that had once been house walls. "Be careful where you walk! And stay out of trouble, if you can!"

"Gee! Are you that tough with your students too?" Caldwell asked as he climbed up behind them.

Gray turned his dour gaze to the rancher. "No, only tiresome reporters."

Caldwell went to Stacie and handed her the camera case. "He must have got up on the wrong side of the bed," Martin said softly so only Stacie could hear.

She did not respond. Gray's moods had always been a mystery to her and everyone else who knew him. She wasn't going to attempt to try to analyze it all now, she thought crossly. Instead she set about exploring the ruin with Martin, who had the decency to at least be civil.

Gray and Dr. Wilmott, meanwhile, went to work, first checking the area against a topographic U.S. Geological Survey map. They examined and collected a sampling of potsherds lying on the surface to take back to the university for further analyses. Dr. Wilmott then brought up equipment from the Jeep, and they set about measuring the ruin with a steel tape, an alidade, and a leveling rod. They began a hand-drawn map of the ruin's structures on cross-sectioned paper on which the measurements were drawn to scale and noted.

By this time Stacie had begun taking pictures of the ruin and the archaeologists at work. She took her time to choose interesting compositions, selecting the right aperture and film speed for each one. Martin observed her closely, asked her to explain what she was doing, and thought of further questions. Stacie did not mind. In fact it was a compliment to have someone so interested in her work. Her co-workers at *American Traveler* took her expertise for granted. And Gray, it seemed, preferred to ignore the fact that she had any special ability.

She went back to her equipment case. A surprised look came over Martin's face when she took out another Nikon camera, similar to the one she had been using, and a collapsible tripod.

"Two cameras?" he said.

At this point Gray and Dr. Wilmott were walking to a part of the ruin less than ten feet away from where she and the rancher were standing. They began measuring the square-walled remains of a one-room structure.

"Yes, I keep one loaded with Kodachrome sixty-four speed for hand-held shots. When I'm photographing moving objects like our two professors here, I need fast film," she said, throwing a glance at the two men. Dr. Wilmott turned his head and smiled at her. Gray, who was pulling out his tape measure, only looked irritated.

She continued, ignoring Gray's lack of response. "But for still scenes, I use a tripod and a slow, fine-grained film to get more sharpness and detail, especially in low light like the shadows of this cave. It's more efficient to keep two cameras loaded with the two types of film."

"I'm impressed!" Martin said. "You've already taught me a thing or two. If it's not too much trouble, maybe you could come by the ranch sometime and look at some of the shots I've taken. You could probably tell me how I might have done them better."

Stacie was in the midst of setting up her tripod, and the suggestion took her somewhat by surprise. She flicked a glance at Gray and saw his jaw clenching, though he did not look away from the notations he was making in a small field notebook.

She was not anxious to see Caldwell alone at his ranch, whatever the pretext. It wasn't that she didn't trust him or didn't feel she could handle him, and it wasn't that she disliked him. But she didn't want him or anyone else to get a mistaken impression. Caldwell thought she was unattached, and she hadn't been blind to his interest in her. She didn't want him to get the idea that she might welcome that interest. And she didn't want to muddy the waters where Gray was concerned. They were murky enough already.

On the other hand she felt the rancher had allowed them all to look at the ruin mainly to please her. That made her feel that she owed him a favor, and critiquing his photography attempts seemed like a suitable return gesture. Perhaps a short visit some afternoon would settle her obligation without creating any difficulties.

"All right," she said after some hesitation. "I don't know how much help I'd be," she added, not wanting to sound too eager.

"When?" Martin asked.

"Well . . . some afternoon?"

"Fine! How about tomorrow?"

"Oh . . . I suppose that's okay," she said, surprised at his rush. *At least we'll get it over with,* she thought. She glanced at Gray, but he had his back to them.

Early in the afternoon they left the ruin. After dropping Caldwell off at the ranch house, they started back to the university, stopping in Wickenburg first for a late lunch. Gray said little and seemed particularly morose. As usual it was up to Dr. Wilmott to try to lighten the atmosphere with innocuous conversation.

Gray spoke directly to Stacie only once. When they were leaving the cafe in Wickenburg, Dr. Wilmott had stayed behind for a few minutes to pay the bill. Gray and Stacie walked out together. They reached the Jeep and he unlocked the door for her to get in. He looked at her accusingly and in an insinuating voice said, "What kind of game are you playing?"

"I'm not playing any game, Gray," she said, startled at the question.

"No? You aren't enjoying pulling the strings and watching two men jump?"

"You're imagining things. And when did you ever jump for me? Only when it suited you!"

"Well, it doesn't suit me anymore!" he said with a gritted jaw.

"Good!" she retorted, blinking back hurt, angry tears. They formed no more than a temporary reddened glaze over her eyes. "Because I don't want you jumping for me if it means I have to conform to your version of the perfect woman."

He stared at her with flintlike eyes. "What the hell does that mean?"

"It means," she said, her lips trembling with restrained emotion, "that if I let myself cry and threw my arms around your neck, you'd be melting all over me. But if I'd try to discuss things with you like an adult individual and not a simpering female, you wouldn't even listen."

He looked at her, his eyes black, almost violent. He swung the Jeep's back door open. "Get in!" he said with grating disgust.

She did, quickly. He slammed the door on her just as Dr. Wilmott was leaving the restaurant. He reached the Jeep as Gray was getting behind the wheel. They drove off. Even Dr. Wilmott did not try to break into the frigid silence that filled the vehicle.

In an hour they arrived at the university. Stacie followed the men up to the archaeology offices to pick up some research material from the library room. As they walked down the hall, Stacie noted with a wary eye that Angelica, Gray's student, was ahead waiting by his closed door. She was dressed in slacks again and another tight-fitting top. As soon as the blonde saw him, she smiled and walked to meet him, her full bosom bouncing gently with each measured stride.

"I was wondering when you'd get back. Have you graded my test *yet*?" she asked in her teasing manner.

A pang went through Stacie when she saw Gray smile down at her.

"Yes, you got an A."

"Did I?" she exclaimed excitedly and clasped his forearm with both hands. "Can I see?"

"Sure," he said, extricating himself from the girl's grasp to get his keys out of his pocket. They walked ahead of the others to his door and he unlocked it. As he did so a key or two fell from his small leather case. Angelica laughed and picked them up for him. As she placed them into his palm she said, "You're always dropping these. I'm going to have to buy you a good sturdy key ring!"

"Do that," he said with an inviting smile as he opened the door to let her in. Dr. Wilmott and Stacie were passing by now, but he took no notice of them. Instead he followed Angelica into his office and shut the door behind him.

Stacie's heart fell with a jolt. Gray had never closed his door when he was in his office. The only time she had known him to do so was the day he first kissed her. Stacie lowered her eyes from the shut door, her face paling.

She felt Dr. Wilmott's hand at her elbow, as if in support. "See you tomorrow, Stacie?" he quietly asked.

It took a moment to find her voice. "Maybe not," she said, pondering. "I'm supposed to see Mr. Caldwell in the afternoon. I was going to borrow a few books from the library room, if that's okay. Maybe I'll just study them at home tomorrow morning."

"Of course. Whatever is best for you." After a slight hesitation, Dr. Wilmott added, "He's different, Stacie, now that you're back. He's alive again."

"Is he?" she said with subdued sarcasm. "Well. I'm glad of that."

The next afternoon Stacie drove alone to the Caldwell ranch. As arranged, she got there about two o'clock, expecting to stay for perhaps an hour or two. Martin Caldwell had other ideas. After showing her his photographs and talking photography with her until five o'clock, he then surprised her by saying that his housekeeper was preparing a dinner for two tonight. He handled it in such a pleasant, graceful manner that Stacie found it difficult to refuse.

They ate dinner at one corner of his large dining room table. Maria, a quiet young Mexican woman who was his cook and housekeeper, served them.

"She's an excellent cook," Stacie said as they were finishing the main course.

"Yes, she's a good worker. Her husband works for me too, as a ranch hand. They live in a small cottage within walking distance of this house. A very nice couple—very happy together." Caldwell paused and added in an ironic tone, "Unlike some of us. You may have heard, I'm divorced."

Stacie was slightly embarrassed with his straightforwardness, but said smoothly, "Yes, I've heard. Your former wife teaches at the university, I understand."

"Yes. Statistics and computer programming. She's a very bright lady. We have a twelve-year-old daughter who lives with her. She's a lot quicker than her old man too."

Stacie laughed. "That can't be true."

"Oh, you'd be surprised. That little girl's a whiz, just like her mother. That was part of the problem, you see. Sue, my wife, is something of an intellectual. I don't know what she saw in me. I graduated college but just barely. I know cattle ranching because I was brought up on it, but the finer intellectual pursuits escape me. But Sue was so bright and quick, I was fascinated by

her. We started out pretty good—lived here and she drove in three days a week to teach. But after a while communication between us gradually broke down. We were just too different, I guess."

He spoke without emotion, but Stacie sensed a wistfulness in his eyes. "How long have you been divorced?" she asked.

"Three years. It was a tough thing to get through. You're young yet, Stacie. Don't rush into marriage. Be sure you're marrying the right person first."

Stacie gave a sad little chuckle. "Yes, I know that from experience. I married before I finished college. We're separated now and will probably be divorced soon." She felt emotion closing up her throat but tried to quell her feelings. Things were not going well with Gray, and she might as well admit the truth to herself: their marriage had little hope of surviving.

"I'm sorry to hear that," Martin said quietly. "Sue and I met when we were both students at college too."

Stacie instinctively opened her mouth to correct his wrong assumption, but she quickly changed her mind. Martin didn't need to know that her estranged husband had not been a student she had met at college, but Dr. Gray Pierce. If he knew, she sensed he might develop an animosity toward Gray which could hinder work at the ruin. She would only be around for a few weeks doing the assignment anyway. There was no need to upset the apple cart. She needed her article and Gray and Dr. Wilmott needed information from the ruin. Let it be, she decided.

CHAPTER SEVEN

The next day Stacie deliberately stayed away from the university again, still feeling hurt and unsteady where Gray was concerned. She wanted to be in control of herself when she saw him again.

So as not to waste the day, she drove down to the Casa Grande Ruin, a national monument about an hour's drive south of Phoenix, to photograph it and study the displays about the ancient Hohokam in the visitor's center. Late that afternoon she phoned Dr. Wilmott and arranged to go with him and Gray in the morning to the Caldwell ruin.

She met them in Dr. Wilmott's office. He, of course, was happy to see her and greeted her warmly. When Gray walked in he only looked at her dourly for a moment as if to say, "Where have *you* been?" Then he ignored her and spoke to Dr. Wilmott. He said not a word to her during the drive to the ranch nor at the ruin as they began their work.

Dr. Wilmott mentioned that Martin Caldwell had some business to attend to and would not be at the ranch that day, so Stacie worked quietly by herself while the two archaeologists continued their research.

They had finished their measurements the day before and had begun to slowly go through the rubble in one of the small, square

106

rooms. It apparently had been a one story structure whose roof and the tops of its walls had long ago caved in. She heard Dr. Wilmott say that Caldwell had pointed out this room as the one in which he believed he had found the clay bird years ago. She watched them on their hands and knees, bringing out fallen rocks which had once served as bricks, and, occasionally, pieces of broken pottery.

Dr. Wilmott had brought a camera. Now and then he would stop to take a picture of the floor of the room from different angles as it was gradually being cleared. These he made a record of.

After a couple of hours, Gray took a break and sat on the ground in the shade of the cave, for it was growing hot as the day progressed. He took out his field notebook and began writing.

Stacie knew, from having lived with him, that careful record keeping was a vital part of an archaeologist's work. She had looked through his field books from other digs and had marveled at their preciseness of detail. Every artifact and feature found was noted and other important data recorded. One side of each page of the small field book was cross-sectioned so that floor plans showing the location of artifacts could be drawn.

At the Archaeology Department library she had seen a cabinet that contained the papers and reports of previous university archaeologists who had died over the long years past. Included with these papers were their field notebooks.

As she watched Gray now, a little distance from her, making notes in his book in his left-handed way, she realized that one day it, too, would be left for posterity with his other contributions. A sense of the finite quality of life invaded her. Her eyes were large and sad as she stood there studying him. She would have liked to have shared his life.

Perhaps feeling her eyes on him, he looked up from his notes. His eyes narrowed, first showing annoyance and then puzzlement. She dropped her gaze and, needing something to do, picked up her camera. After hesitating a moment she self-consciously brought it to her face. Aiming it in his direction, she found him in the viewfinder and began to walk toward him. He was watching her. After a few steps he took up the right amount of space in her viewfinder to make a good composition. With graceful, featherlike movements of her fingers she refined the focus.

He was still watching her in his brooding way. She lowered the camera from her face. "Don't look at me. Go back to your writing. I want to get the dedicated archaeologist at work," she told him, her heart rate increasing because it was the first time she had spoken to him all day.

His shoulders dropped slightly as he exhaled in annoyance, but he did as she instructed. She thought she even saw a hint of a smile on his face as he bent his head to write. Her camera clicked.

In spite of this tiny thaw between them, he paid no further attention to her while they remained at the ruin. In early afternoon it was growing too hot to work, so they quit for the day. As before, they stopped at a café in Wickenburg for a late lunch.

Gray was quiet. Playing it cool, Stacie decided. Dr. Wilmott began asking her how her article was coming. As she discussed it with him, she mentioned she had photographed Casa Grande and would need to get photos of other ruins in the area.

"Gray, didn't you say you had to go to Tonto tomorrow to check their new display at the visitor's center?" He turned to the younger man sitting next to him in the booth.

"Yes."

"Is that one you'd like to get photos of, Stacie? Maybe you could go together," Dr. Wilmott suggested. "Gray could give you first hand information while you're there."

I'm sure he'd love that, Stacie was thinking. She didn't know what to say. She wanted to go with him, but didn't want to force the issue. Like Gray, she decided to play it cool.

"Well, I wouldn't want to interfere with his work. I can go there on my own sometime."

"What do you think, Gray" Dr. Wilmott asked.

Gray, who was maintaining a poker face, shrugged a bit. "It's okay with me," he said as if he didn't care one way or another.

"Well then, it's settled," Dr. Wilmott said complacently.

Stacie smiled slightly for Dr. Wilmott's benefit but avoided looking at Gray. She put her hands in her lap beneath the table, not wanting anyone to see they were shaking.

Later they arrived at the university parking lot. Gray chose a time to pick her up the next morning and asked her to give him her address, which she did. He handled this in a very businesslike way and Stacie didn't want to stir up tensions again by suggesting they meet at the university. Besides, her condominium was in the direction they would be going, and meeting at the university would not have been convenient.

They parted like distant acquaintances and Stacie walked to her car. As she was pulling out of the lot, she saw Gray on the steps of the Archaeology Building. He was talking to Angelica.

He picked her up in the Jeep the next day as planned. Dressed in old, well-fitted blue jeans and a short-sleeved plaid blouse, she waited outside for him and got in when he pulled up. They exchanged subdued greetings, then drove for a few minutes in silence. She ventured to ask why he had come in the Jeep. Gray explained that part of the way they would be traveling was unpaved. This was the sum total of their conversation until they were well out of the city and driving through the foothills of the Superstition Mountains on Apache Trail Road.

The paved two-lane road wound into dry, rocky hills sparsely covered by desert shrubs interspersed with saguaro, yucca, and cholla. After a while they passed a sign that stated they were entering Tonto National Forest. Now and then along the way were small signs warning that they were passing through a flash flood area. As the road kept climbing, Stacie found she had to swallow occasionally to clear the pressure in her ears.

The total silence between them was wearing on her nerves. "You had something to do with preparing the display at the visitor's center?" she asked finally.

"Yes, I helped update their information and worked with the display artist. They're about to set up the new display and wanted me to check it."

Well, he managed to put two whole sentences together, she thought waspishly. Deciding to press her luck, she spoke again. "How long will it take to get there?"

"About two more hours, maybe less."

She said nothing more. After a few minutes had passed she was surprised when he spoke again. "I thought we'd stop at Tortilla Flat for lunch. We'll be there in about an hour. Is that too early to eat?"

"That's okay. What's Tortilla Flat?"

"It's a tiny town, geared for tourists. Used to be a stagecoach stop. There's a café and small hotel there and a livery stable. Want to go horseback riding?" He flicked a glance at her, his eyes amused.

He *would* laugh, Stacie thought dryly. They had once gone riding together on a weekend trip, and she had fallen off the horse. "No thanks," she said.

After a few silent moments, Gray said, "A lot of time has passed since those days."

Surprised at the remark, she raised her eyes to look at him.

He turned briefly to meet her gaze. "Have you been happy in New York?"

Her heart began to beat more rapidly. Was he finally willing to discuss their situation? "Happy enough." She tried to keep her voice light.

"So you like life in the big city?"

"Yes."

He nodded his head slightly, his eyes on the road again. "Women seem to," he muttered.

It made her recall Dr. Wilmott's story of his old girl friend. Overcoming inhibition, she decided she had nothing to lose at this point by asking him about it. It was a whole part of his life she had known nothing about.

"I heard once that you . . . that when you were a graduate student you . . . wanted to marry someone else?"

His brown eyes turned to her sharply. "Where did you hear that?"

She smiled a little. "It doesn't matter. Is it true?"

His eyes went back to the road and he was quiet for several long moments.

"Yes, it's true. Why are you asking about that now?"

Her complexion reddened slightly. "I thought . . . I was wondering if it had anything to do with our breaking up."

He gave her a curious glance, then put his eyes back on the road. "Nothing at all."

"You weren't still in love with her . . . or . . . or anything?" She swallowed, realizing how vulnerable she sounded. And felt.

She watched him smile. "All that was over about a dozen years before I met you."

His casual reply made her relax. She was afraid he was going to say he had still been in love with the other woman. It would have been a plausible explanation of why he had let Stacie go so easily: she couldn't compare to his former lover. She was relieved it wasn't true.

"How come you didn't marry her?"

"Because while she was still pretending interest in me, I found out she was playing around with other men."

"Was that after she went to New York?" she asked.

He glanced at her again. "I see you got all the details."

"Not really. How did it happen? What was she like?"

He smiled. "My you're full of questions!" His eyes pondered the road for a moment. "She was a successful local model, beautiful and vivacious. The type who likes to be with an exciting crowd and in the limelight. I wasn't the only man who was taken with her. I was young and didn't want to recognize that she wasn't the type to settle down. I'm not sure what drew her to me."

Stacie was surprised at this statement. He must realize how

111

attractive he was with all the female students who had crushes on him.

"Anyway," he was continuing, "I wanted to marry her. She agreed. But first, she said she wanted to go to New York for six months to try her luck at big-time modeling. I didn't like it, but I knew I couldn't stop her. She was very strong-willed. So she went to New York. Six months stretched into a year. We stayed in touch and she kept saying she'd come back to Phoenix. Finally I went to New York to see her and found she was living with a man. That finished it."

"You never saw her again?"

"Only on fashion magazine covers," he said dryly. "She did become a top model."

"You must have been terribly hurt," Stacie said.

He moved his head slightly but didn't answer.

Stacie mulled all this over for a few minutes, then asked, "Were . . . were you having an affair with her . . . before she went to New York, I mean?"

He glanced at her momentarily. "Why do you need to know that at this late date?"

Her color heightened. "I . . . I don't know. I never really knew much about your past."

He gave a slight sigh. "Yes. I had an affair with her."

"Oh . . ." The thought of him making love to someone else, however long ago, stung her. She knew she shouldn't have asked.

He turned to look at her bent head. "Is that significant to you?"

She swallowed and made herself meet his gaze. "You didn't want to have an affair with me. Instead you rushed me off to Las Vegas. Why?"

He shifted his eyes back to the highway and took a while before answering. "You were a lot less experienced. She wasn't innocent when I met her. You had virgin stamped all over you. And I was so much older than you. I told you then, didn't I, that I was afraid of taking unfair advantage of you? Every time I touched you I felt like a dirty old man."

112

"That didn't last long," she muttered with dry humor.

He glanced at her, a little startled. She was surprised to see color rising under his tan. "No. Once we were married I lost my guilt feelings," he admitted, a trace of self-directed amusement in his tone.

"Was that the only reason we hurried to Las Vegas?" she asked.

He stared ahead and was silent. She thought she could guess why he did not answer. Since speaking with Dr. Wilmott a suspicion had formed in her mind about Gray's reasons for rushing her.

"You knew I was supposed to go to Denver that weekend for a job interview. Did that have something to do with it?" she prodded him. "Were you afraid *I* would leave town and never come back, like your model?"

He was negotiating a curve. He opened his mouth as if to speak but then closed it again.

A glaze came over Stacie's eyes. "That was it, wasn't it? You rushed me into marriage that weekend so I wouldn't take the interview—to keep me from a career."

His profile was growing stern. "All right, it's true. I didn't want a repeat of the past. But I tried to warn you," he said, turning a hard glance at her, "to think carefully before going ahead with the marriage. You were so eager, you didn't think twice. I tried to make you see marriage was a serious commitment."

"I took it seriously," she said. "I was so anxious to marry you I didn't care about the interview. I didn't realize your marrying me was a tactic to keep me from getting a job!"

She looked at him accusingly, but he kept his eyes on the winding road, his mouth grim. "You wouldn't have needed to trick me, Gray," she went on. "If I had got that job, I would have come back and married you. I could never have hurt you the way your model did. . . . But I suppose you wouldn't have been sure of that," she said, a note of empathy in her voice. "And when I finally got a job—when I took the assignment in Alaska—I *did* come back to you!" Her eyes and voice emphasized the positive meaning of her words.

He responded with anger and resentment. "You came back. Eager to leave on another assignment as soon as you could! You call that a serious commitment to our marriage?"

Stacie stared at him, baffled. He was carrying on as if she had not been faithful to their marriage vows. It seemed he had missed her point, that she wasn't like his model. *She* had been true to him. Couldn't he see that?

She said nothing more. Seeing Gray's hard feelings had been awakened again, she didn't want to chance another long, angry silence.

In about ten minutes they came upon a set of rustic buildings on the right. There was a wide gravel parking area in front and Gray pulled in. Her eyes widening a bit, Stacie looked over the group of wood structures, all of which looked as though they had been constructed of old used boards from other buildings. Some of the individual boards were painted in various colors and were interspersed with unpainted ones to create a look that was purposely makeshift. In front hung a large, hand painted sign that said: TORTILLA FLAT, POPULATION 6, ESTABLISHED 1853. RESTAURANT, SALOON, SOUVENIRS, HOTEL.

He parked in front of the central building. There was a small U.S. mailbox in front and a sign on a window that read POST OFFICE. They got out of the Jeep and climbed a few steps, passing a colorfully painted wooden Indian, to an open door.

Inside was a curio shop, crowded with display cases and browsing tourists. In back was a long bar made of thick, heavily varnished wood with leather upholstered bar stools running along it. To the right of the bar and extending back was a small dining area crowded with tiny tables covered in red and white plastic cloth. All around from the ceiling and wood-plank walls hung old bottles, branding irons, wagon wheels, old tubs and cooking equipment, harnesses, and other antiques associated with the Old West.

There was a table for two free in the far corner, and they

threaded their way through the cramped quarters to reach it. The table stood by a long picture window which looked outdoors onto cactus, a strip of abandoned railroad track, and a darkly comic arrangement of old trunks, a headstone, and a dressed dummy asleep in an antique wheelchair.

When they had taken their seats in front of the window, Stacie turned to look at the setting again. "This place is sure different!" she said, breaking into a grin.

"It has atmosphere," Gray agreed with a smile, leaning back in his wood chair. Stacie was glad they were being distracted from their moody quarrel.

A waitress soon came and handed them menus. They ordered Cowboy Cheeseburgers and sarsaparilla. Two bottles of sarsaparilla were brought a few minutes later, with Kerr's canning jars filled with ice to serve as glasses. Stacie laughed a bit as she tried to drink from the ridged rim of the jar.

Gray was watching her with an odd half-grin. "It never did take much to entertain you."

She looked at him and smiled, not sure what he meant. Light from the window behind them highlighted the amber tinge of his brown hair. He blinked slowly in a pensive way. In a voice that simply stated a fact, he said, "I never thought you would need such an exciting job to keep you happy."

Her smile faded and her face grew sad and thoughtful. "It's not that I need the excitement so much, but I do love photography and I want a successful career at it."

He nodded his head slightly and his expression became closed again.

"I suppose I was too young when we married, wasn't I?" she said. "I didn't foresee that . . . that there would be problems."

"Yes, I knew you were too young. I was afraid you'd get . . . bored. And I could see," he said rather self-consciously, "that you were a good photographer."

"You never said so," she interrupted in a hushed voice, surprised to hear him admit it now.

He smiled ironically. "I didn't want to encourage you. I

figured some magazine would eventually offer you a job that would mess up our lives. I managed to distract you from going to Denver, but I could only elope with you once. What happened was inevitable, I suppose."

Stacie chewed on the inside of her lower lip before asking the next question. On a half-breath she said, "Do you still want a divorce?"

His eyes were sharp for a fleeting moment, but then his expression was passive. "If you do. It doesn't matter much to me, as I have no intention of marrying again. If you want one, you file for it."

Stacie felt let down by his reply. She was hoping he might suggest they try again—he had said he wanted her back a few days ago. She supposed he had now decided their situation was hopeless.

Maybe he was right, she admitted, trying to accustom herself to the heartbreaking reality. They didn't seem to understand one another. And apparently he didn't want to live with her new, career-minded self. She was surprised he never wanted to marry again. Did Angelica know that? she wondered. Was he settling for an affair with her?

When lunch was finished they left to drive on to Tonto National Monument. Just as they were leaving Tortilla Flat the road dipped when they crossed a dry stream bed. Signs near the road said TORTILLA CREEK and DO NOT ENTER WHEN FLOODED.

"How did it get the name Tortilla?" she asked Gray out of curiosity.

"From the flat pancake-shaped rock formations around here," he replied, lifting his hand from the wheel to point out the window.

"I see. It's a nice place," she said wistfully, knowing she would be nostalgic about it once she got back to New York.

The sense of sad finality stayed with her all the way to Tonto. The paved road turned to gravel soon after leaving the small town. That and sharp, ascending and descending hairpin curves

116

made the going slower. At last they pulled into the parking lot at the national monument. She browsed around the visitors' center exhibits and watched the slide presentation while Gray was on business in the center's offices.

She was bending over a mano and metate left out for visitors to examine when he came out. She remembered the stones—one small and hand held, the other much larger with a lengthwise trough—were used by ancient Indians for grinding corn.

"Why don't you try it?" she heard Gray's voice behind her.

She looked up and smiled. "All right," she said. She kneeled down and picked up the mano. A small bag of dried corn was sitting nearby for visitors to use. Gray bent to scoop some up and threw the kernels onto the metate. She rubbed the heavy brick-like stone over the corn in the trough but made little progress toward grinding it into meal. When her arms were tired she laughed and put the stone down. "I give up," she said and stood up again.

"If you had been an Indian girl living in a pueblo you'd have to do a better job than that if you expected to get married," Gray said. "A bride-to-be had to go to her fiance's house and grind corn for four days in front of his mother to prove she'd make a good wife. If the amount of corn she ground wasn't satisfactory, the marriage was called off." He told her all this with some amusement.

"The good old days when women knew their place, Gray? Too bad you didn't live then!" she said, keeping her voice light. "What about divorce? Or didn't it exist? I suppose women were stuck for life grinding corn for their husbands." They had begun to walk outside now to start the steep trail up to the cliff dwelling.

"No, actually divorce was quite simple," he said.

"They threw the wife off the cliff?" she suggested innocently.

"No. They had a matrilineal society, which meant that the women owned all the property. If a wife wanted to divorce her husband, she just put his personal belongings out of her house while he was out hunting or working in the fields. When he came back, there was nothing he could do about it. If the husband wanted the divorce, he just collected his things and went back to his mother's house."

Stacie smiled at the idea of women holding all the property rights. "Obviously a superior society," she commented with a subtle humor.

"Thought you'd like it," he said dryly.

The trail was paved but very steep. Large cumulus clouds were dominating the sky, but the sun was very hot. Momentarily out of breath, Stacie paused to adjust the camera bag she had over her shoulder. Before she knew it, Gray had come up, taken it from her, and slung it over his own shoulder.

"I can carry it," she protested in a soft voice.

He shook his head. "Men are still stronger than women, you know—all other things being strictly equal, of course," he said with a little glint in his eye.

It warmed her heart that he was joking with her. She looked up to find him watching her expression, his eyes alive with amber lights reflected from the sun. Finding herself a little diffident suddenly, she looked away.

This was crazy, she was thinking as they continued on. A while ago the atmosphere between them had been so heavy. Now, though she had scarcely been aware of it, their moods had shifted. *How long would* this *last?* she wondered. Did it mean there was hope for them? One thing positive she had noted: He was no longer attempting to treat her like a child. Stacie found her spirits soaring and it gave her new energy to finish the climb.

They took the last steps up and came to a ruin in a cave somewhat larger than the one on the Caldwell ranch. She got out her camera and set to work taking pictures. It became difficult because clouds began blocking the sun often, varying the light just as she had made the proper adjustments on her camera. Gray watched her work and answered questions that came to her mind.

The Salado Indians who had built the ruin, he told her, had a culture that blended Anasazi and Hohokam traits. They practiced irrigation in the broad valley below, working peacefully alongside the Hohokam. The Tonto ruin had been built in the early thirteenth century and was abandoned in the early 1400s.

"Do you think the Caldwell ruin was built about the same time?" she asked as they were descending the trail back to the visitors' center.

"Probably," Gray said. He sounded distracted and she noticed he was looking at the darkening clouds.

"You think it will rain?" she asked, watching the changing cloud shadows move over the panoramic valley and hills that the ruin looked down on.

"I'm afraid it may." He sounded worried. "We'd better hurry along," he said, putting his arm around her waist to help her keep up with him. It was growing windy and her hair blew into her face.

"I've heard it's been dry. Don't we need the rain?" she asked, trying to be nonchalant about the fact that he was touching her. Her heart was beating faster and she felt happy to be so close to him.

"We need the rain, but I'd prefer it didn't come while we're out in the desert. I'm glad I took the Jeep."

"Why? What's the matter?"

"Have you forgotten everything about living in this part of the country? When the ground has been baked hard in the sun for a long time, it means there could be flash floods if there's a sudden heavy storm. The water doesn't soak into the ground fast enough and it runs off in torrents down the creek beds. Cars and people have been known to get swept away."

"Do you think we'll be all right?" she asked with concern as they reached the Jeep.

He looked up at the sky. "If we're lucky it'll hold off for a few more hours."

It didn't. They were on the gravel road turning along the steep edge of a deep canyon when the skies broke. It was only a few heavy drops for some minutes, but soon they were engulfed by a downpour. Gray had to stop at one point because the rain was so thick he couldn't see out the windshield. For a while their ears were assaulted with the sound of thunder and hail pelting the Jeep's roof.

"What should we do?" she asked. "Turn around and go back?"

"I can't turn around here," he said. "It won't be any better back there. We have to try to make it to Tortilla Flat. It shouldn't be too far from where we are now."

The storm let up a little and he moved ahead. Stacie looked out the side window and could see water flowing in the bottom of the canyon. It had been dry on the way out. Before too long they came to a dip in the road and stopped. A fast flowing stream of muddy water covered it. Ahead, Stacie could see the wooden buildings of Tortilla Flat.

"The sign said, 'Do Not Enter When Flooded,' " she reminded Gray. "Should we cross it?"

Anxiously she watched him look about, surveying the situation. The stream at present was not too deep, though the waters were flowing fast. "I'm not too crazy about sitting here," he said, his hands clenched on the wheel. "We've got four-wheel drive and heavy tires." He looked at her. "You want to risk it?"

"It doesn't look that bad," she said, glancing again at the water moving over the road. "The rain's stopping."

"Hold on tight!" He changed gears and they moved ahead. They entered the fast flowing waters and could feel the pull of the current on the vehicle. But the Jeep held steady and soon they were across. They drove the short distance to the parking lot and stopped.

Gray let go of the wheel as though his fingers were stiff. He looked at Stacie, his color a shade lighter than usual. "Well, we made it."

As she was smiling at him a sound of rushing water caught her ear and she turned to look out a rear window. She gasped. "Gray, look!"

The dip they had just crossed was now covered with a high raging torrent of churning water. Had they been in the road now, had they hesitated a minute longer, they would have been hit by a literal wall of water.

She felt weak for a moment and put her hand on Gray's arm. He looked at her, his eyes a little hollow from shock. "We might have been killed," he whispered. He put his arms around her and held her close. She buried her head in his shoulder, recovering.

In a little while he gave her an extra squeeze. "Come on, darling, let's go in." He kissed her forehead.

She nodded, noting somewhere in her dazed mind that he had called her darling.

It was still raining. Gray hurriedly got out of the car and ran around to her side to open the door. She picked up her bag of camera equipment and stepped out. She tried to shield her face from the sudden wetness that hit like a cold washcloth. It brought her to her senses. All at once only one thought was in her mind.

"Wait, Gray!" she said, taking her camera out of the bag. "I've got to get a picture!"

"Of what?"

"The flood water." She turned to call the words back to him, for she was already running toward the still rushing stream.

"Stacie!" she heard him yell, but paid no attention. She was almost near a rocky outcrop by the stream and next to the road. The rain was increasing again, but she no longer was aware of getting wet. She was about to climb the rocks when she felt herself gripped about the middle and pulled back.

"What are you doing?" she said in surprise and annoyance, fighting him.

He kept hold of her squirming body. "Those rocks are slippery! You'll fall in!" he shouted in her ear.

"I'll be all right! Let me go!" she yelled back, angry now.

She felt him dragging her away. "Come on inside and don't be silly! You don't need a damn picture!"

"Yes, I do!" she said, clenching her teeth. She turned within his grasp to face him and tried to push against him. "I need it for the magazine! It's my job!" The more she struggled the

121

tighter he held her. She threw her heel back, took aim, and kicked him in the shin with the toe of her shoe.

"Ouch! That's it, little girl!" he said in rage. Keeping his crushing grip on her shoulders, he reached down and brought his other arm under her knees, lifting her off the ground.

"Put me down!" she screamed. "You . . . you bully!" She beat him about the shoulders, but it had little effect except to make him grimace.

He carried her all the way to the front steps of the café-curio shop. There he set her down and snatched the camera from her hands.

She was breathing hard and trembling with fury. "You'll regret this, you. . . . Where's my camera bag?" She looked and saw it sitting by the Jeep where it had been dropped. As she made to run toward it, he grabbed her.

"I'll get it! Go inside where it's dry!" he ordered.

She made an effort to get at her camera again, but he held her off. In the next moment he had twisted her sideways. Holding her against him he delivered a swift swat of the hand to her posterior. Before she could yell he was pushing her inside the door.

In spite of being wet her face and body felt sweltering hot. The room was a blur as she heard the door close behind her. She had never in her life felt so enraged. Her eyes didn't focus and she felt as if steam must be rising from her heated skin. She stood there breathing heavily and using all her willpower not to start throwing the books and souvenirs on display all around her.

Now she heard the door open and close. She knew it was Gray and deliberately did not turn around. Vengeful ire began to erupt in her again and her temples began to throb.

"I put your camera and the case in the Jeep. It's locked up safe," he told her. She felt him take her arm. "C'mon let's . . ."

She turned on him. "Don't you touch me!" She was shaking and her voice was like a hiss. Yanking her elbow out of his grasp, she backed away from him like a cat who's had its paw stepped on.

Gray stayed where he was, his hair wet and water streaming down his face, looking vaguely perplexed, as if he did not know quite how to proceed. He eyed the frail, trembling woman in front of him, her soaked clothes clinging to her soft curves, her dark hair hanging close about her face in dripping ringlets, and her green eyes blazing with hatred for him.

He started to say something and then apparently changed his mind. Then, as if making some inner resolution, the uncertain expression on his face changed and his eyes grew firm. "We have to stay here for the night, if we can," he said quietly with authority. "I'll see if they have a room."

Suddenly anxiety was in her eyes along with wrath. "I'm not staying here with you!" she said boldly. Underneath her bravado she knew that if that was what he wanted, she had no choice in the matter. She had no way of getting out of Tortilla Flat on her own.

Now Gray's face was dark with resentment. "Maybe we can get two rooms," he said, acidly biting out the words. "We have no choice but to stay here. There will be flooded areas all the way back to Phoenix. It's too dangerous to travel now."

"I hate you for this!" she said.

His mouth curled angrily. "I didn't ask for the rain!" Eyes black and determined, he moved past her to the cash register by the wood bar.

The place was empty at the moment and he hit the bell on the counter to call for service. Stacie warily moved in range to hear him negotiate for rooms. *He had better get two,* was the only thought in her head.

A friendly looking man came out from a door in the back. "Hello!" he said brightly, looking at Gray and then Stacie. "Sorry, I didn't realize anyone had come in. Get caught in the rain?"

"Yes," Gray said in a voice that sounded thinly restrained. "Do you have any vacancies for the night?"

"You're lucky! I have one room left, a double. That suit you?"

"Yes," Gray said grimly. He turned and caught Stacie's scathing glare.

"Name please?" the proprietor said as he opened a registration book. A hesitance in his tone indicated he was beginning to sense the tension in the atmosphere.

"Pierce," Gray said.

"That's ah . . . Mr. and Mrs.?" he asked, eyeing them both a little nervously.

"Can't you tell?" Gray replied with heavy sarcasm.

The "hotel" had only four rooms as it turned out. A second-story facade had led Stacie to believe it was larger. Their room was neat and clean and included a small kitchenette. In spite of the homeyness of the place Stacie's eyes burned when she saw the double bed. She eyed the small sofa opposite it, under the front window.

"I'll sleep on the couch," she announced, her expression set.

"I'll take it. You can have the bed," Gray said.

"I don't need any self-sacrificing from you!" she all but shouted at him.

"All right, I'll take the bed then!" he yelled back.

For a few minutes both ambled restlessly about the room. There was no luggage to unpack and nothing to do but not talk to each other. Stacie considered taking a shower to rinse off the stickiness from the rain, but the thought of having to put on her damp clothes again made the idea seem futile. She did grab a towel from the bathroom to blot the excess wetness from her hair. When she came out she found Gray sitting by the tiny kitchen table. He looked up at her.

"It's five o'clock. We might as well go and eat," he said with a tedious sigh.

The café where they had eaten lunch was almost empty now. Only one small family was there occupying a table near the bar when they walked in. Gray and Stacie moved automatically to the table by the long window, where they had sat earlier in the day.

Gray ordered a steak dinner and a Coors. Stacie asked for a

124

salad. When he admonished her that she ought to have ordered something more substantial, he got a withering look.

"What, are you going to be mad at me all night? I didn't plan this!" he said.

"You had no right to stop me from taking that photograph!"

"I probably kept you from breaking your neck," he replied with barely tethered patience. "Or getting washed away. You've got enough photographs to send back to your damn magazine."

"That's not for you to decide!" she snapped back, eyes ablaze. "And I can take care of myself. I don't need any of your damned chauvinistic protectiveness!"

"Good, I'll remember that!"

The rest of the dinner was eaten in fuming silence. When they got back to their room, Stacie took a shower and wrapped herself in an extra sheet from the closet. She hung her damp clothes to dry over one of the kitchen chairs. That finished, she took a pillow from the bed and stretched out on the couch to go to sleep.

"It's only seven thirty," Gray said, looking up from a paperback he had bought before leaving the curio shop. He was sitting in an easy chair near the bed.

"What else do you suggest I do?" she asked sarcastically. She watched his eyes move over her blanketed form as if visualizing the smooth, soft, feminine body underneath. She glowered at him again, her skin hot with anger and something else. She turned over and faced away from him into the back of the couch.

In a while she heard him get up. Her heart began pounding as she felt his footsteps come near to the couch. But he continued on and soon she heard the shower running. When he came out, the lights went off and in a few moments she heard him getting into the bed. It was dark now and all was silent.

She relaxed, exhausted physically and mentally. Her anger had quieted and it left her feeling weak. In a while she was asleep.

In a few hours, she wasn't sure how long, she awoke again. The short couch made her feel cramped and she turned onto her back hoping to find a more comfortable position. She tried to go back to sleep but now found she was wide awake. Looking over at the bed in the darkness, she could make out Gray's long form under the covers. Moonlight was coming in through a gap in the draped window above her.

She sighed. Somehow she knew it would be a long time before she could fall asleep again. After lying still for a while, then trying to squirm into new positions hoping to find a comfortable one, she finally sat up. Pulling up the sheet to keep herself covered, she leaned over the back of the couch and pushed the inside edge of one drape aside to peek out the window.

The rain had stopped. The sky was full of stars now, and moonlight gave a pale quiet light over the desert landscape. The road and parking lot were empty except for the Jeep and a few other parked cars. Dark puddles of water still lay over sections of the graveled area. It seemed a still, silent world, far removed from the one which had brought her life so much turbulence during the day. The argument over the photograph of the flood waters seemed far behind.

She heard a movement on the bed and turned to look. She saw Gray lying on his side now, facing away from her. The covers had slid down and his smooth back and broad shoulders were uncovered, their strong contours outlined by the dim light. When she found herself wanting to run her hands over those hard sinewy muscles, she quickly turned her head away.

Looking out the window again, she found tears blurring her vision of the quiet world outside. *How had it all come to this?* she wondered. It had been so beautiful when they were first married. Now all they could do was argue. How had she lost him? Just because she wanted a career? Was there some crime in that? She had been true to him. She had loved him. Still loved him . . .

Her face crumpled. She sniffed softly and wiped the tears off her face with her hands.

"Can't you sleep, Stacie?"

She stiffened. His voice was very near. She had been so caught in her own emotion she had not heard him get up.

She kept her face averted. "I'm all right. Go back to sleep."

She felt his weight sinking into the sofa cushions just behind her. Then she could feel the heat from his body warming the skin of her bare back.

"I can't sleep either," he said. She could feel his breath in her hair, and the softness of his low voice at her ear keyed up all her senses. "I've been awake all night."

She said nothing, not knowing how to respond. When he moved a little closer, she tensed. She could feel the thick soft hair on his chest brushing lightly against her back. Her arm was resting over the sofa back's squared edge. In a moment his arm came to rest on top of hers, his hand closing around her small fist.

By now her heart was thudding against her ribs. "Don't Gray," she whispered.

"Don't what?"

"Don't touch me!" she said brokenly.

"Why not? You used to like it. You still do, I think." His other hand was moving over her slender shoulder now in a light feathery touch. She felt goose bumps rising over her arms and back. "There's a way we could both get to sleep, Stacie."

"No!"

"That's not a word you ever used to say," he softly chided. "Sometimes you used to come to me and ask me to make love, in your shy little way."

"Stop it! Don't talk about it!" She tried to move out of his reach. His hands gently grasped her upper arms, and he forced her to turn around on the couch and face him. Her cold fingers clung tightly to the fabric she held over the front of her body.

"I think we should do more than talk about it," he whispered, rubbing the warm, slightly rough palm of his hand up and down her arm.

She knew she ought to get up and walk away from him, but his touch and voice were hypnotic. Her limbs felt weak. "If we're getting a divorce, we shouldn't. . . ."

"Are we?" His voice rose above its whisper now. "That's up to you. Why should what we do here tonight matter? We're two people who used to make love very well together. Why shouldn't we now? We both need it—that release of tension. It's why we can't sleep."

"You're very clinical about it all," she said bitterly.

"*You're* talking about divorce—a legality! What's our enjoying each other on a sad, lonely night got to do with anything? Who would know? Who would even care?"

"I would!" she said, looking up at him for the first time.

His face was dimly lit; his eyes very dark, but with a brightness from within that made her take in her breath when she gazed at him. "I'm glad to hear that," he said in an odd tone. He stared at her for a few long moments, his eyes shimmering with determination and need. He took his hand from her arm and brought it up to stroke her cheek and long neck with his fingertips. "Don't you want to know if it can still be like it used to be? Remember how we used to lie together, Stacie? Embracing one another . . ."

"Please stop!" she cried, unable to stand it anymore. She put her hands to her face, covering her eyes. In the next moment he had taken her in his arms, her face and hands against his shoulder. She felt him pull the sheet away from her, felt the cool air on her skin, felt her vulnerability to his caresses. She knew she was lost.

She trembled as he stroked the length of her back, one hand gliding down over her hip and thigh. Her skin quivered at his touch. She put her tremulous hands around the back of his neck and buried her face next to his throat. She kissed the warm skin.

"Oh, Stacie!" His voice was low and urgent. His hand moved up her rib cage, deliberately brushing against the side of her breast. She shuddered in his arms and gave a soft cry of pleasure. His hand slid over her breast then, completely encompassing it in gentle, tactile warmth, squeezing, stroking, caressing.

She had gone too long without his touch. Already she felt out of control. His fondling ignited a fire within her that would burn mercilessly until it was quenched. She writhed against him and brought her lips near his mouth.

128

His hard, glittering gaze rested on her upturned face for an instant, as if he meant to devour her. Then he fastened his mouth upon hers and his embrace tightened. The air was pushed from her lungs in his firm hold, her soft breasts and nipples pressed against his heated chest. She returned the kiss with all her strength, opening her mouth to him, letting him ravage her.

After long delirious moments she pulled her head back to get her breath. Both were breathing heavily and unevenly. "Gray, oh, Gray," she urgently cried, her body aching now to have him. His hand began to move purposefully down her body, over her smooth abdomen and soft stomach. She stopped his hand before it could reach its destination. She was already on the brink. Her eyes were wild with need as she looked up at him. "Gray, yes . . . make love to me. . . ." Her voice was husky and pleading. The words were unnecessary, for he already was lifting her in his arms.

She put her arms about his neck as he carried her, kissing with love-moistened lips the tender, heated skin beneath his ear. Her hands caressed the strong column of his neck, feeling the smooth masculine skin with curious, sensual fingertips.

He reached the bed and laid her upon it. With her hands clinging around the back of his neck she urged him toward her, not wanting him to hesitate even a moment. She was thankful there were no clothes in the way to delay them. Obliging her, he eased himself down on her supple form, pressing her into the soft pillow and sheets. He made no further move to possess her yet, but rather lay on top of her, caressing her, as if to absorb the very essence of her.

It was marvelously good being held beneath him, bearing his weight, feeling his skin warm and urgent against hers. Like old times. She felt as if her heart were breaking with joy. It was what she had dreamed of, reversing hopeless, longing memories of all those nights alone in New York. Her lost husband and lover, back again . . . here . . . now . . . loving her. For a moment the intensity of her emotion seemed to paralyze her throat, making

129

her unable to breathe. As she caught air back into her lungs in a convulsive gasp, the sound resembled a sob. Perhaps it was.

"Stacie," Gray answered, his own voice choked. "You feel so good to me! Why did you stay away so long, damn you!"

"Pride . . . thinking you didn't want me. I don't know . . ." she said breathlessly, her mouth against his shoulder, kissing the firm, smooth skin while her tremulous, seeking hands stroked his back.

"No," he murmured. "I have only myself to blame." He moved so that his thigh rubbed the inside of hers. The sensation devastated her. She wanted to complete their union now, quickly. A hollow ache within her yearned for his fulfillment. Her heart thudding, she grasped his small, firm buttocks as his thigh muscles began to move against her rhythmically. She thought she would go crazy.

"Gray, please," she said, her voice a gasp, a whisper. "Please don't make me wait anymore! Please . . ."

As she urged him to her, he became a part of her. She felt herself near delirium. At long last she experienced that wondrous, comforting sensation of being filled. She had gone so very long without it, without him. She wanted to weep with the intense pleasure of it.

But she could feel Gray's need now was very urgent and she wanted to respond to him, experience it with him. And so, together, as they had used to do, they moved in their own private rhythm, their natural harmony creating a delicious burning sensation that smoldered, then inflamed her. All she could do was cling helplessly to him, for he had taken over. She reveled in, wanted to absorb the masculine strength and tension in his body as he moved against her and with her. Unconsciously her arms pulled him as tightly to her as possible, as if wanting her body to permanently fuse with his, so that they would be one being forever, not two halves of a whole which could become separated again. She knew they must never, never again be parted.

Soon the tension his loving was creating within her had reached an unbearable level. She was gasping in small, shallow breaths and arching her neck, her chest pressing upward into his. A high aching gasp escaped her as the final fulfillment came, and as she clung to Gray tightly, she felt his deep, shuddering response in her arms.

Afterward, as his muscles relaxed, she felt him melt over her. Gently, lovingly, she stroked his back, murmuring his name.

He moved to one side and pulled her to him so that they lay in each other's arms. "My sweet, sweet Stacie," he whispered. His hand was at the back of her head, his long fingers buried in her curls. She felt him reverently kiss her cheek then nestle her head against his neck. Stretching slightly, she pressed her lips against his skin in a loving nuzzle then fell asleep.

In a while she awoke when she felt him move in his sleep. He had turned and was lying half on top of her, one arm curled carelessly over her waist. She smiled. It was a pleasant feeling to be half-pinned beneath him. Her eyes were still heavy with sleep, but she lifted her head for a moment to gaze at his long, reclining, uncovered form.

She had always thought him particularly well built—broad back, narrow waist and hips, tight buttocks, and muscular legs. He always seemed so unaware of the physical beauty he possessed, either not wanting to capitalize on his looks, or not realizing that he could have easily used them to gain an advantage.

Sighing comfortably, she stroked her hand over the relaxed muscles of his shoulder and arm resting on her chest. She moved her fingers toward his face, touching the smooth, angular cheekbone dimly highlighted by the thin stream of moonlight that crept through the draped window. Such a handsome face, she thought; strong, yet at times so gentle.

Softly she touched his closed eyelid with her fingertip, then pushed her fingers luxuriously into his hair. She turned slightly toward him as she did so and felt her breasts brush against him. The soft burning sensation began to steal over her and she realized she wanted him again. She leaned closer and lightly pressed her mouth close to his, afraid she would wake him and yet hoping she would. Suddenly her mouth was engulfed by his in a warm kiss. He lifted his head and peered down at her in the darkness.

"What's this? Can't you let a man sleep?" he teased softly.

She wanted to think of some clever answer for him, but couldn't. She was too comfortable and sleepy to be witty, or to concentrate on anything but what she wanted most at that moment: To seduce him.

"No," was all she said, but she said it in an inviting little voice.

"No?" he said, smiling down at her. "Again, Stacie?"

"Yes," she breathed. As she reached to put her arms around his neck, he grasped her tightly about the middle and turned onto his back so that she was on top of him. She laughed lightly, clasping his shoulders to steady herself.

He moved his hands caressingly over her back, from the softness of her derriere over the small of her back and up toward her shoulders. She braced her hands against the pillow beneath his head and lowered her lips to his. While he tasted her mouth, he glided his hands to the sides of her back near her breasts. With his thumbs he reached between their touching bodies to stroke her nipples. Soon her breaths had grown shallow and she was making small gasps of desire.

In unspoken accord they moved to become one again. Stacie pressed her lashes together in rapturous pleasure at the sensation. Once more they moved in a natural unison, ages old, this time in a more languid way, stretching the loving out as long as they could.

At last she could take no more. The taut thread within her was ready to break and she was beside herself with the need for release.

The final moment came like white lightening. She cried out in the terrible ache of pleasure. Gray was grasping her roughly in the throes of his own passion, and she dug her fingers into his taut, muscular shoulders. A wave of cold suddenly passed over her and for an instant she felt as if she could lose consciousness.

132

It quickly passed, but the realization of how strong her response to him could be was frightening.

But now the beautiful haze of relaxation came over her and she felt warm and tired. She pushed herself to his side and cuddled next to him as he lay on his back, exhausted.

"Will you let me get some sleep now?" he said in a softly amused voice before pressing his lips to her forehead.

"Yes," she said with a gentle laugh. She nuzzled her head against his shoulder and languidly draped her arm across his chest.

In a few more minutes she was asleep.

CHAPTER EIGHT

She opened her eyes the next morning to find Gray sitting up next to her. Blinking lethargically, she thought she had never slept so soundly. He was watching her, his expression pensive, his eyes moody.

"Good morning, sleepyhead," he said, his mouth quirking into a slight grin.

She smiled and stretched, then sat up next to him, against the headboard, pulling the covers up with her. "What time is it?"

"Nine o'clock."

"Oh, no," she said, amazed she had slept so late. "How long have you been awake?"

"An hour or so."

An hour? she thought, studying his somber profile. An hour he had apparently spent pondering while he watched her sleep. She leaned against him and reached out to touch the hollow beneath his high cheekbone.

"My beautiful, brooding professor," she whispered slowly, enjoying the sound of each syllable.

He looked at her, a quizzical expression passing through his eyes followed by a patient grin. "You're silly," he chided her as the grin faded.

No, she wasn't, she thought as she rested her head against his shoulder. But he wouldn't understand, and that was just as well. If he began to realize how other people saw him, he might change, and she didn't want that. She loved him for his brooding nature. His voice interrupted her silent contemplation.

"I hope we don't have to wait another two and a half years to wake up together again." There was an edge to his quiet voice that demanded a response.

"Of course not . . ." she began to assure him, but he didn't let her finish.

"We should be together, can't you see that?" His voice was growing sharp.

She gazed earnestly at his profile, for he was not looking at her despite the determination in his words. She sensed some part of him was afraid of her reply. "Of course I can, Gray."

He turned and looked into her eyes. His voice was husky. "Then why don't you come back to me?"

Instantly her eyes filled with tears. "I will . . . if you want me," she answered in a small voice.

She had never seen so much emotion in his face; he looked almost pale with relief. He took her in his arms and his voice was nearly breaking.

"Of course I do! I never really wanted a divorce, Stacie. I only used it as a threat to try to keep you with me. When it didn't work, I gave up. I thought you wanted that job because you were tired of me."

"You were so wrong, Gray!"

They held each other for a long moment. Then, as if to be sure, he asked, "You'll leave New York then? Move back to Phoenix and live with me?"

After a second's hesitation she said, "Yes, I will." *It would take some working out,* she was thinking. But she didn't see why she couldn't live in Phoenix and still work for *American Traveler.* She might have to fly to New York fairly often, but she could handle most assignments over the phone with Ben. Since she was the magazine's best photographer, she felt they would be willing to make some concessions. In other respects her job would be the same. She would simply make Phoenix her home base and mail in her photos, which she often did anyway when she was away on assignment. It could be worked out, she decided.

He was softly kissing her neck now and she pulled away from him a bit. There was something she had been wanting to tell him and now was the right moment. "Gray," she said with a tremulous smile, her hands on his shoulders, "there hasn't been anyone else, while we were apart. You're the only one I've ever let make love to me."

He smiled and she thought she saw a mist in his eyes. He held her to him again and kissed her. "I was afraid to ask," he told her in a hushed voice. "I've been alone too. No one could replace you."

Two tears spilled from her eyes as she pressed her cheek against his shoulder. She had been worried about him and Angelica—about other faceless women as well—and was overjoyed to find out there was nothing to her fears.

They clung to each other for some time, the sheet she had pulled up to cover her having fallen away some time ago. Her soft breasts were against his chest and she could feel his hands growing more caressing over her back. All at once he took her by the shoulders and pushed her away so he could gaze at her.

"You're beautiful, Stacie," he said, his eyes traveling over her delicate face, frail shoulders, and small breasts. She smiled and lowered her eyes from his ardent look. On their wedding night she remembered she had been filled with anxiety that he might be disappointed with her frail body, especially her small bosom. She had quickly been shown, of course, that all her worrying had been for nothing. Even so, she still found it reassuring to know that her small frame appealed to him.

His hand slid from her shoulders to touch her breast, gently pressing his fingers into its yielding contours. His touch made her take in her breath suddenly; her eyes winced sensually. "Gray," she said, halfheartedly pushing his hand away. "We ought to be getting back to Phoenix. Dr. Wilmott may be waiting for us to go to the ranch."

"We won't get back in time to meet him anymore. Not since you wore us out last night and made us sleep late."

"*I* wore us out!"

"Who attacked whom in the middle of the night?" he asked. She smiled and he watched her blush. "You're not quite so shy as you used to be."

She supposed she wasn't. Two and a half years of independence changes a person. "You didn't seem to mind," she said, still playfully fighting his groping hands.

"Far from it!" he agreed with a small grin, his eyes growing more and more predatory. "How about attacking me again?"

"But Gray," she protested, giggling as he began to push her down onto the mattress, "poor Dr. Wilmott . . ."

"It's his own fault. He suggested this trip, didn't he?"

A few hours later, Stacie stepped out of the bathroom feeling refreshed after a shower even though she was wearing her rain-wrinkled clothes from yesterday. She saw Gray, dressed and ready to go, sitting on the edge of the bed. His head was inclined in a contemplation, but he looked up when she came to him.

She reached out to touch his hair. "What are you brooding about now?" she asked lovingly. She was so happy herself, she couldn't understand the somber look in his eyes.

He took her hand and kissed the palm, then looked up at her. "Are you sure you're not going to mind quitting your job?"

"Quitting . . . my job . . ." Her voice trailed off as a sense of foreboding set in. "But I won't have to. I think I'll be able to live in Phoenix and still keep my job at *American Traveler.*"

He let go of her hand. His eyes widened and he paled slightly. "I thought you meant you'd give it up. You still want to travel?" he asked in a thin voice.

"It's my career. You didn't really expect me to give it up, surely? I told you what it means to me."

His expression was becoming very grim and she was beginning

to tremble. They had just found happiness again; they couldn't be losing it already. Over this!

"More than our being together, obviously." He got up and walked a few paces away from her.

She began to think he was being very unfair. "Why is it my job that has to be sacrificed to have more time together? I don't see you offering to give up your career to be with me."

He turned sharply and glared at her. "You're the one who travels. I stay in one place!"

Well, so what? she thought, feeling the old bitternesses coming back. "Why do men feel it's the woman's duty to make all the adjustments? Many women have husbands who travel because of their work. They accept the situation. Why can't you?"

"If I were a woman," Gray answered acidly, "I wouldn't marry a man who would be away all the time."

"If you were a woman! If you were female you'd stay home cooking and cleaning all day because you think that's all a woman's supposed to do!"

He took a long breath and exhaled it as if trying to keep his patience after being insulted. "Gender doesn't have anything to do with this. A person can either accept long separations or he can't. I *can't*. I want my wife next to me not off in Timbuktu!"

"You want a convenient sex partner, you mean," she muttered harshly, feeling suddenly as if she had been used.

He stared at her for a moment, as if pondering the route to her brain. "Stacie, why do people get married? Isn't it so they can be together every day? I always thought that was the reason. Didn't you?"

As she looked at him, her eyes grew confused, slightly vacuous. She opened her mouth but couldn't form any reply.

"Pretty words," she finally said in a weak voice. "It's all just pretty words. If you loved me you wouldn't ask me to give up something that means so much to me." Her expression sharpened. "In all the pretty things you told me last night and this morning, you never said you loved me."

"I showed it!"

"I don't equate sexual arousal with love," she said in disgust. "But I don't think you ever knew the difference. All you've ever seen me as is a plaything. You married me so you wouldn't feel guilty about having sex with me and to keep me under your thumb! You never loved me! You never even said you did!"

He stepped toward her looking like he could readily shake her to pieces. "Don't talk about love to me!" he said in a harsh guttural voice. "You don't know the meaning of the word!" His face was flushed and vindictive. "I'm not going through this again. I wash my hands of you! If you don't get that damned divorce, I will! And then I don't ever want to see or hear from you again. I don't want to know you exist!"

The veins in his neck were protruding and he was shaking with rage. For the first time she was afraid he might do something violent, but in a moment he was gone, slamming the door behind him.

She sat down on the bed trembling, feeling faint. Her mind seemed empty for a few minutes. But at the realization that she had just lost him again, she buried her face in her hands and began to sob almost hysterically. After a long while her spasm of uncontrolled emotion passed, and she told herself she must pull herself together. There was still the ride back to Phoenix to get through, that is if he hadn't driven off and left her there. How thankful she would be to get back to New York! How grateful she would be to forget all this!

After drying her eyes and trying to compose herself, she walked outside. The Jeep was still parked in front, but she did not see Gray. She assumed he must be inside having breakfast or something. After spending about fifteen minutes idly waiting, she grew impatient and decided to find him.

As she'd suspected, he was sitting at the bar in the café, a cup of coffee in front of him. Warily she approached him. When she came up to the empty bar stool next to his, he turned to glance at her. She felt a trace less anxious when she saw he looked much calmer now, though there was no tenderness in his face.

139

"You want breakfast?" he asked curtly. If he noticed her swollen, reddened eyes, his hard expression did not indicate it.

She shook her head. "When will we leave?"

"When I'm finished." He took some change out of his pocket and laid it on the counter, apparently to leave as a tip.

She said nothing. Assuming he would be finished soon, she stood where she was, waiting. After a few minutes he seemed annoyed. "Why don't you sit down or wait outside?"

"I'm tired of waiting. I'd like to get out of here," she said, putting some toughness into her voice. She didn't like his treating her as if she weren't there.

"Well that's too bad. I intend to get a refill," he said, picking up his half-full cup. "Why don't you go outside and sit on the bench by the wooden Indian," he said as though trying to rid himself of a bothersome child.

Burning hot tears filled her eyes. For some reason the words and his dismissive tone were more cruel than anything else he'd said. She picked up a quarter from the change on the counter, threw it in his coffee, then turned and rushed out.

She waited by the Jeep, shaken with nerves and a feeling of humiliation. He came out a few minutes later. She expected him to be angry again, but he appeared stoically in control. He unlocked the door for her, and they drove back to Phoenix in absolute silence.

CHAPTER NINE

The next few weeks were a strain. With the exception of brief, impersonal exchanges Gray and Stacie did not speak to one another at all, even though they were together most weekdays as work continued on the Caldwell ruin. It seemed to Stacie that Gray had accomplished his wish to forget she existed.

Dr. Wilmott seemed aware of the frigid atmosphere between the couple but did not comment on it. She wondered if he could guess what had happened at Tortilla Flat but knew he would not ask. It seemed the department head, after setting things into motion, had decided to let nature take its course without any more assistance from him. If things did not work out between the troubled pair, as obviously they were not, Dr. Wilmott probably did not want to be blamed. So he kept a tactfully oblivious eye to it all.

The daily routine was altered quite a bit when Martin Caldwell, at Dr. Wilmott's respectful suggestion, magnanimously allowed the professors to have two archaeology students at the dig to help speed their work. Two were quickly chosen: Tom, a boyish, pleasant-looking first-year grad student, and Angelica.

No doubt they were chosen by Gray, Stacie decided the morning the students first appeared to join the daily Jeep ride to the

141

ranch. From then on, instead of having the Jeep's backseat to herself, Stacie was obliged to share it with them, though Tom was occasionally absent.

Angelica, however, didn't miss a day. Stacie listened to her chatter and the way she teased Gray until she wished she could tape the girl's mouth shut. As the days grew hotter and hotter, Angelica often wore short shorts and brief tops over her well-endowed curves. When Tom was around he could hardly get any work done for ogling her.

Gray did not seem oblivious to her feminine charms either. He joked with her, smiled at her, left himself open for her flirting. Stacie noticed he never touched her, even casually, but she assumed he had to keep some professorial dignity about him. Angelica had no such qualms and often gave him suggestive touches on the arm, which seemed designed to provoke even more than her words. And when they drove back to campus after a day's work at the ruin, Angelica would invariably go with Gray back to his office. Tired of watching them together, Stacie would usually head straight for her car and her condo.

At first Stacie had thought that Angelica was just a sexy little man-chaser who looked upon the methodical, aloof Professor Pierce as the supreme conquest. But at the ruin, while she was working with her camera or talking to Martin, she observed that Angelica was often watching Gray while he was engrossed in his work. She saw a vulnerable, longing look in the girl's eyes that indicated she saw more in Gray than just a conquest. Stacie was familiar with the symptoms: Angelica was falling in love. She didn't know whether to feel sorry for the girl or tear her hair out. She tried not to care.

Work progressed faster with two extra pairs of hands. Stacie often joined in too, under Dr. Wilmott's direction. Even Martin lent a hand in the digging and sifting for tiny pieces of ancient pottery, cloth, and tools.

As evidence of unusual Aztec influence increased, Stacie called New York to ask Ben if she could spend more time on the assignment than originally planned. After explaining the promising finds they were uncovering he gladly allowed her to stay. She was the only reporter on the scene, an invaluable advantage should something extraordinary be unearthed.

Stacie told herself she was glad for the sake of her assignment but knew underneath it was more her masochistic need to be near Gray even though it hurt her. When she finally left for New York again, it would be for the last time, and that she found unbearable to contemplate. And yet, after seeing him smiling at Angelica, she would often tell herself she couldn't wait to get back to New York. *Let him start an affair with her!* Stacie would think. She didn't care anymore.

One day at the ruin, Stacie found herself working with Angelica, sifting through soil with a screen. Tom and Martin were not around that morning, and Gray and Dr. Wilmott were looking over a room at the other side of the cave. As they sat on the ground working together, Stacie carried on small talk with the young blonde, noticing the girl kept eyeing her in a speculative sort of way.

"Do you and Gray not like each other or something?" Angelica said all at once.

"Why do you ask?" Stacie replied cautiously.

"Because you never talk to each other. And sometimes, I . . . see him looking at you."

"It's true. We don't get along well."

"Why?"

"Oh . . . it's a long story," Stacie said with a smile, continually surprised by the girl's forthright manner. Angelica always seemed to feel she had the right to say anything.

Angelica was quiet for a few minutes, poking through the bits of matter that had been caught in the screen, looking for tiny artifacts. Then she said, rather slyly, "You know, I heard once that Gray's wife had left him, and that he was getting a divorce."

Stacie pretended to be casual. "You knew he was married?"

"Well, he wears a wedding ring."

Both were silent again for a few moments.

143

"When he gets his divorce," Angelica said, "I intend to be the one to pick up the pieces."

Stacie felt the blood draining from her face and she tried to keep her hands steady as she worked. "He's much older than you," she pointed out in as controlled a voice as she could.

"I don't care about that. I think he's sexy! If he only knew . . ." She stopped as she looked up at Stacie and caught her fearful expression.

Stacie consciously hardened her eyes. "Why are you telling me all this?" she asked.

Angelica's eyes grew wary and bold. "Because sometimes I think there's something between you and Gray. I wanted you to know that I've got my mark on him."

Stacie suddenly felt very adult in the face of Angelica's obvious immaturity. "There is something between us. I'm his wife." She watched the shock passing through Angelica's blue eyes. "And I think you ought to grow up a little before you try to take him on. You might get your fingers burned."

She was surprised to see Angelica smile securely. "Trying to scare me off? If you're hoping to keep him, you must not be getting very far if you're not even talking to each other! I'm not worried about my ability to handle him!"

Stacie wet her lips, shaken by the girl's confidence. Trying to put a similar confidence into her own voice, she said, "You don't know everything about the situation. Gray and I are still sleeping together," she said, knowing she was stretching the truth a great deal.

She watched Angelica straining to keep her expression from revealing any alarm. A vindictive light entered the girl's eyes. Her pink-frosted lips trembled slightly as she jeered, "He's been sleeping with me too!"

Stacie could not hide her shock. She stared at the triumphant expression on the girl's face and wondered whether to believe her. At Tortilla Flat Gray had told her there was no one else. Had he recently started an affair with Angelica out of spite? Or

144

was the young blonde just saying that to make Stacie give Gray up?

She wasn't sure but feared the worst. Repugnance and hurt welling up inside her, she got up and walked away, pretending to go back to work with her camera equipment. In a few minutes she glanced over at Gray and Dr. Wilmott. They were hard at work, unaware of anything else. Her eyes pondered Gray's broad back as he was bending over a shovel, as if to ask, "Oh, Gray, is it true?" Then her troubled eyes caught Angelica's smug smile and she thought she would be ill.

She was grateful to see Martin driving up a few minutes later in his Land Rover. After hurriedly repacking her equipment she picked her way down the steep slope, sliding part of the way, because she always had trouble keeping her footing on it. She met Martin, who had waited below when he saw her coming down. After telling him she wasn't feeling well—because of the heat, she explained—he offered to drive her back.

She had remained on friendly terms with Martin and had even been to his ranch once more for dinner at his invitation. But she had been very careful not to appear too friendly, and the rancher seemed to sense and respect her distance.

After her conversation with Angelica, however, she welcomed the rancher's friendship more openly. She was always glad when he came to the ruin after that, for it gave her someone to talk to besides Dr. Wilmott, who was usually busy. She was alienated from both Angelica and Gray now, and she had little in common with Tom. Martin's calm, considerate nature and his genuine admiration for her work kept her feeling that she had some value as a human being.

Probably sensing she was letting down her defenses where he was concerned, the rancher was quick to take advantage. He began asking her to the ranch more and even driving into Phoenix to take her to dinner at some of the city's fine restaurants. While he made no overt moves, no physical advances to scare her away, he began in subtle ways to make it clear he was growing fond of her.

It was around this time he threw a casual, rather impromptu party. He showed up at the ruin one day and asked them all to come up to his ranch Saturday night. A little later he had quietly asked Stacie if she would mind coming early in the afternoon on Saturday to help him get ready. She agreed, not realizing that it would lead to her acting more or less as his hostess when the guests began to arrive.

On Saturday evening Martin took care to personally introduce her to each of his friends as they came to the door. And when he was busy getting drinks for his guests, he asked once or twice if she would answer the doorbell for him.

And so it was that when Gray appeared at the door, alone, Stacie let him in. He seemed taken off guard for a moment, so much so that his voice faltered when he said hello to her. Martin came up then to greet him and shake hands. During their brief interchange, Martin lightly put his hand on Stacie's shoulder and then took her with him to check on the hors d'oeuvres.

Stacie was surprised that Gray came at all. He had never been a party-goer. Dr. Wilmott and his wife were already there, and a while later Angelica had arrived with Tom. At first Stacie was relieved to see her with Tom, thinking it meant the girl was bluffing about her relationship with Gray. But after Gray arrived things quickly changed. Angelica made a beeline for him and he hung about her the whole evening.

Angelica was wearing a low-cut top over her slacks, and she was clearly enjoying Gray's unconcealed gazes at her generous cleavage. His leering at the girl made Stacie feel not only sick, but also inadequate. She was wearing a casual yellow cotton dress. It had a V-neck that on a more well-endowed woman might have looked sexy. On Stacie it looked trim and demure.

Tom, meanwhile, took an interest in the pretty daughter of one of Martin's ranch-owning friends. Stacie began to think Gray and Angelica had planned it that way. After all, they would have the same problems as he and Stacie did when their romance began. Students weren't supposed to date their professors. Gray couldn't have actually taken her to the party himself.

So she came with Tom, a convenient friend who didn't care if he was shed, so she could spend all her time with Gray.

By late evening Stacie had a terrible headache from the tension of trying to look relaxed and cheerful while watching Gray with Angelica. She apologized to Martin for not staying later and left at the same time as some of the other guests. When she walked out, Gray was sitting with Angelica alone in a corner. He was casually tugging at the ends of her long blond curls as they softly talked, Angelica looking up at him adoringly.

The following Monday, Stacie wanted to chuck it all and go back to New York. Instead she masochistically showed up at the Archaeology Department to go to the ruin with the others. She found Angelica looking particularly pleased with herself that morning. No doubt she had had a pleasant weekend. Gray's expression, as usual, revealed nothing.

It was a tedious day, lightened only by Martin's brief appearance. He asked to take her out to dinner later that week and it brightened her spirits a little.

At the end of the day they went back to the university. Stacie had decided to take home a book she had used at the library, so she went up to the Archaeology Department offices with the others. On her way back from the library room she noticed all the others were in Gray's office, searching about. Angelica was on her hands and knees on the floor, and Gray was looking under his desk.

"What's the matter?" she asked Dr. Wilmott.

Dr. Wilmott was bending slightly to peek under a chair. "Gray dropped his key holder, and the keys scattered all over. He's still missing a couple."

Stacie left, figuring Gray probably wouldn't welcome her help anyway. She went back to her condo, made herself a sandwich, then took a shower to clean off the dust from the dig. After putting on her short nightgown and a lightweight robe, she settled down to study the book from the library.

In an hour or so she was surprised to hear the doorbell, for she was expecting no one. She wished now she had put on a pair of slacks instead of lazily throwing on her nightgown, so she wouldn't have to change again.

She went to the door and cautiously looked through the peephole first. She saw Gray. A wave of panic swept through her. Why was he here? What did he want?

She opened the door. "Yes?" she said, putting a hard edge in her tone.

Gray looked a little disgusted. He still had on the dusty jeans and blue shirt he had worn all day. *He must not have been home yet,* she was thinking.

"I lost my house key at the office this afternoon. We couldn't find it anywhere. I was wondering if you still had yours?"

She lowered her eyes coolly. "Yes, I'll get it for you."

She left him at the door and went into the bedroom. Opening up her suitcase in the closet, she reached into one of its pockets and took out a folded handkerchief. She opened it and looked at its contents: A house key, a much smaller key, and a gold wedding band. She had purposely brought them with her, though she wasn't sure why at the time she left. Perhaps she had hoped she might need them again.

When she stood up she found he had come in and was watching her from the bedroom door. Clutching the handkerchief in her hand, she walked up to him. She opened her palm and unfolded the cloth.

"The house key," she said, picking it up and giving it to him.

"I'll have a copy made. . . ." He started to say.

"I don't want it back! This was my key to the safety deposit box." She handed him the smaller key. Looking at the remaining item for a moment, she forced herself to pick it up and extend it to him. "You might as well take this too. You paid for it. The gold must be worth something."

His jaw clenched and there was a movement in his throat. His eyes were huge and quickly becoming red-rimmed. "You make me hate you sometimes!" His voice sounded cruel and broken. With a rough movement he pushed her hand away. "I don't care what you do with it but don't give it back to me!"

She turned from him and put the ring on her dresser. *What right did he have to sound so injured?* she thought with deep resentment. He was the one who had taken up with someone else! Why did he act now like a hurt and rejected lover? *Did* he love her after all?

She turned and looked at him. He was putting the keys in his pocket. He met her gaze with wrathful, liquid eyes. "How can you be so cold-hearted after what happened at Tortilla Flat?" he asked in a savage whisper.

"How dare you bring up Tortilla Flat! All you did was use me!"

"*Use* you?" He was moving toward her, his facial muscles taut. "You wanted to make love as much as I!"

"You call it lovemaking, but there wasn't any love in it, was there?" she challenged him. Let him deny it. Let him tell her he loved her, if he did!

He stared at her dangerously, saying nothing. He looked as though he might wring her neck, but instead he pulled her roughly into his arms. His mouth crushed hers, pressing her head back. His tongue ravaged the honey-soft interior of her mouth and with his hands he pushed the lightweight robe down her arms until it fell to the floor at her heels. As she tried to move out of his grasp he drew her closer, his hot, searing mouth leaving hers to travel down her chin to the sensitive skin of her throat and down to the silken valley between her breasts. She whimpered in her struggle against the sheer strength of him. But at the moist feel of his lips and the rough, caressing hands roving over her back, she began to breathe more deeply. She wanted to respond to him, and she knew she mustn't.

"Stop it!" she said as firmly and unemotionally as she could, trying to keep the breathlessness out of her voice.

"You know you don't want me to." He murmured the words into the hollow where her neck met her shoulder before gently biting the soft, white skin.

"Stop it!" she cried, more frantically this time.

He paid no attention. He pushed the strap of her nightgown

off her shoulder, and it proved traitor to her, sliding easily down her arm and completely exposing her breast. His hand quickly rose to fondle the soft, newly exposed skin, while with one strong arm he kept her pressed close against him. Her shoulder and head were locked against his rough denim shirt. The dust from his clothing and his masculine scent filled her nostrils. She told herself she must get away from him before he got the better of her, and at the same time she felt she was already slipping, for she didn't want to be out of his arms.

She was beginning to feel sensually mesmerized. His whole body seemed overheated from anger or arousal or both. His fingertips, hot and trembling, deftly found their way to her nipple and stroked it seductively. The heat of his hand on the sensitive, rose-colored skin sent shock waves through her. She could feel her breast swell under his touch while her nipple grew small and budlike. He bent his head to take it gently in his lips and tease it even more with his tongue.

She softly groaned in sweet agony, unable now to keep herself from responding. His mouth came back to hers, now gently invading her lips already parted on a soft gasp of pleasure. The kiss he forced upon her yielding body was long and deep and she became languid in his arms. He lifted his head slightly, keeping his lips hovering an inch above hers. "Let me spend the night with you again," he whispered urgently.

The words jolted her and brought her a step back to reality. A part of her wanted desperately to give in to him, to try to recapture what happiness they had briefly found together. But she knew it wouldn't last. They would only argue again afterward, and she would hate herself and him for having allowed it to happen. She had to face the fact that he didn't love her; he only loved being in bed with her. And hadn't he found a replacement?

"Why? Isn't Angelica available tonight?" she said, bitterness flashing in her eyes as she pushed away from him. She managed to put a few inches between them, but his hands held at the back of her waist.

His gaze took on a hint of smugness. "Jealous, darling?"

"Don't . . ." She was going to object to his calling her darling but found the objection was needed for something else. He had slid his hands to her hips, to the panties that matched her short nightgown, and he was pressing her provocatively against his pelvis, wanting her to feel what could be hers for the asking.

"You have no reason to worry about her," he said with some bemusement at the expression on her face. "You can give me everything I want, Stacie. And you know it!"

"Gray . . ." she said uneasily, trying to push away again. He wouldn't let her.

"Shhhh," he whispered into her ear, his warm breath making her wince. "Come to bed with me again, and everything will be all right." She shivered in ecstasy as his hand moved down her stomach, probing beneath her bikini panties.

Her mind was in turmoil. She wished she were young and gullible enough to believe that if she slept with him, it would solve everything. But that day had passed, and she knew it. She couldn't let herself be seduced by him, or by her own needs. She had to be tough. And coldhearted.

Again she tried to wrench herself out of his grasp, but he held her too tightly. Gritting her teeth, conjuring up all her reserve strength, she forced herself to be rigid. Making her voice firm and unequivocal as granite, she told him, "I don't believe in sex without love!"

She watched his expression and saw the light in his eyes fade and die. Slowly he took his hands away from her. It was a moment before he spoke. When he did, his voice was cool but uneven. "You've made yourself very clear." His eyes seemed to be made of glass now, as she had seen them once before, years ago. He stared at her another moment then turned and began to walk out.

After several paces he paused and looked back at her. "Caldwell's no good for you, you know. He's a decade older than me. You'll be bored with him in no time." He lowered his eyes then walked out.

She stood where she was, alone and confused. For a short moment he had looked brokenhearted. Yet, if he cared, he might have said he loved her, and he hadn't. Perhaps he was just let down, momentarily depressed at having lost a comfortable bed partner. The thought chilled her. But she had known that was how he looked upon her all along, ever since they separated. She shouldn't let the proof of it get to her. And yet, she wanted to hope she was mistaken.

Late that night she finally fell asleep, telling herself she shouldn't hope for anything anymore.

The next day any vestiges of hope she had had left were snuffed out in an odd incident. She had arrived at the university a little earlier than usual and saw Gray drive into the parking lot as she was getting out of her car. She kept her pace slow as he got out of his Jeep, and he caught up with her as they neared the parking lot entrance on the way to the Archaeology Building. He said nothing and neither did she, as if by some silent mutual assent they thought they ought to walk together because they were headed for the same place, but found no necessity to try and converse with one another.

A car drove by on the narrow street. Stacie was surprised to see Gray wave at the woman driver. It wasn't anyone Stacie recognized. As she slowed her car to turn into the parking lot, Gray retraced a few steps and walked toward the woman. She stopped and rolled down her window when she saw him approaching.

"Dr. Pierce, isn't it? I haven't seen you in a while," she said with a polite smile.

Stacie took a few steps toward them and stood a little distance behind Gray as he said, "Not since the last faculty meeting, Mrs. Caldwell. How's the Math Department?"

A slight shock went through Stacie at learning the woman's identity. She stepped sideways a bit so she could get a better look at her face as she was answering Gray's question.

Mrs. Caldwell was a handsome woman: delicate facial structure, dark hair attractively streaked with gray, and intelligent dark eyes. She spoke in a refined, cordial manner and in general appeared to be somewhat more sophisticated than Martin Caldwell.

"By the way," Gray was saying, turning toward Stacie for a moment, ". . . this is my wife, Stacie."

Self-consciously Stacie stepped closer and said hello.

"Actually, we're about to be divorced," Gray added casually —so offhandedly that it came as an affront to Stacie.

"I'm sorry," Mrs. Caldwell murmured.

"Well, it seems to happen to us all, doesn't it? Incidentally, we've been working at the ruin on your husband's ranch. Perhaps you've heard?" Gray said in the same careless manner.

"Martin did mention something one Saturday when he came to pick up our daughter. I . . . didn't pay much attention," Mrs. Caldwell answered. Stacie sensed that Sue Caldwell was also a little uneasy with Gray's conversation.

"Stacie is a magazine photographer. She's been up at the ruin almost every day photographing our work. Martin seems to have an interest in photography, and Stacie's been giving him some help with it. Haven't you, Stacie?" Gray said, turning suddenly to Stacie, a smile on his face.

"Y-yes," Stacie said, giving a weak grin to Mrs. Caldwell. The woman in the car was staring at her expressionlessly, though there seemed to be a tautness in her eyes. Stacie glanced at Gray to give him a sharp look, but he had turned toward the car again.

"So you see, everything works out. Doesn't it?" There was a sardonic tinge in Gray's tone now. "Well, I won't keep you, Mrs. Caldwell. Nice seeing you again." He started to walk away. Mrs. Caldwell nodded a good-bye, put her car in gear, and drove on.

"Why did you say that?" Stacie asked, hurrying to catch up with him.

"What?"

"That . . . we were getting a divorce and . . . and all."

She was at his side now and he turned to look at her, a complacent expression on his features. "Well, we are. Aren't we?"

"Do you have to tell people like that? So cold and nonchalant . . . to a . . . a stranger?"

"People might as well know. They'll find out from the gossip anyway. What do you want me to do? Look sad and grave and wring my hands? Or act as though I can't stand the sight of you? That would be a little ridiculous since we're seen together so much. I'm just trying to be modern and sophisticated about it all, darling. No one looks upon divorce as a serious thing anymore. Or marriage either, for that matter." Gray's voice had taken on a sardonic twist at the last remark.

"Why have you started calling me darling all the time?" she said with annoyance. "You never used to call me that." Indeed, the first time she had heard him use the word was when they realized they had narrowly escaped the high flood waters. He'd said the word with deep emotion then. Now he kept making the endearment sound like a taunt.

"Just to show there're no hard feelings over our divorce . . . darling."

Stacie gritted her teeth at hearing it again, but let the subject drop. "Why did you tell her about me . . . about us working at the ranch?"

"Since she used to live there, I thought she might be interested."

"But . . . you didn't have to mention that I was giving Martin help with his photography. She might have . . . misunderstood. . . ."

"Misunderstood? You haven't exactly been covering your tracks with him, you know. You played hostess at his party. I've even heard that you two have been seen out having dinner together. Sue Caldwell must have heard gossip too. So now she knows who he's seeing. That's all. I wouldn't worry about it. She's been divorced from him for several years. She's probably past caring."

He said all this as though he himself were past caring. In spite of his admonition last night about Martin not being good for her, today he almost seemed to be giving her his blessing. Stacie felt

154

sick at heart. He didn't even care enough to show regret about their failed marriage. All he could do was make flippant remarks. He didn't love her, not at all. He obviously never had.

She couldn't face spending the day at the dig, watching him with Angelica. When they got up to the Archaeology Department, she quietly saw Dr. Wilmott alone for a few moments. She told him she had come down that morning to let him know she would be away for a few days, photographing other ruins. After this little prevarication she went home, packed her suitcase, then drove out of Phoenix.

She stayed away for almost a week, traveling on her own to Montezuma Castle National Monument, Walnut Canyon National Monument, past Flagstaff to Wupatki National Monument, then east to Canyon de Chelly National Monument, and into northern New Mexico to Chaco Canyon. In each place she spent time photographing the ancient remains of a past civilization, all the while trying to pull the remnants of herself together.

When she saw Gray again, when she finally had to part with him for the last time, she wanted to handle it with some modicum of dignity. She didn't want to try to remain friends with him. But she at least hoped to be able to wish him all the best and mean it, and to be able to say it gracefully and without humiliating emotion. A mature adult, she told herself, can walk away from a love which is not returned and can learn from the pain.

CHAPTER TEN

She came back to Phoenix with several rolls of exposed film and a mind steeped with philosophic high intentions. When she went to the university the next morning she found the usual group meeting to go out to the Caldwell ruin.

Gray looked at her darkly and muttered that he'd heard she'd been away. She gave a little smile and said something innocuous, successfully handling the encounter with equanimity. No more accusations and stinging replies, she had decided. She would behave as kindly as she could toward him and not allow herself to be drawn into any more arguments. She would walk out like a lady.

Dr. Wilmott was cordial as ever. "Something rather important has happened while you were gone, Stacie!" he told her as they all walked down to the Jeep. "Gray suspected there might be a burial in one room at the ruin which appeared to have been sealed up. We opened it up, and, sure enough, there was a skeleton and a great deal more."

"Like what?" Stacie asked with growing excitement. Gray was walking with Angelica a little ahead of them but appeared to be listening to their conversation.

"Some good remnants of cloth—the room had been sealed off

so well, it remained dry enough to keep it from deteriorating. Fragments of baskets, some plain, some coated and painted. There was one covered with a mosaic of turquoise and other stones. There are about twenty-five pots. We haven't even got all of it out and to the lab yet."

Angelica laughed. "How could we with Gray hovering over everything? He takes a hundred pictures everytime he removes a speck of dirt from something." The girl looked up at Gray to see how he was taking her teasing. Stacie couldn't see his reaction.

"Archaeologists are like that, Angelica," Stacie said calmly, resisting the urge to make come more pungent remark.

"Of course," Dr. Wilmott said with mild reproof to Angelica. "Burials can yield a great deal of information about the customs of the people. Every detail on the position of the skeleton, its condition, and the articles buried with it have to be recorded before they're removed from the site."

"I know. I was just kidding," a chastened Angelica said. "It's just that Gray gets so finicky about it all, so engrossed he forgets everything else."

Poor Angelica was being ignored, Stacie was surmising. He slept with her at night and forgot about her during the day. Well, she'd have to get used to that, Stacie thought sourly. Apparently the girl hadn't learned yet just what place females had in his life.

"Stacie's comment was accurate, Angelica," Gray said with biting sarcasm. "She's been around archaeologists enough to know we're a pretty boring lot."

Angelica listened to this with a smile and flicked a triumphant look back at Stacie. Stacie managed to ignore it.

"But you haven't told Stacie the most important part," Gray continued, turning to glance at Dr. Wilmott.

"Why don't you tell her?" the older man suggested.

They were outside now and came to a halt by the Jeep. Gray looked down at Stacie. "A lot of jewelry was buried with the skeleton: beads, bracelets, ear ornaments, and . . ." he paused significantly, "a large pendant that is unquestionably Aztec.

157

Similar ones have been found in temples unearthed in Mexico City."

Stacie's eyes widened as she looked up at him. "What do you think it means?"

Putting his hands at his hips, he shifted his weight onto one leg. "I have a new theory for you, Miss Smythe: An Aztec trade merchant, hoping to extend his trade route, leaves the familiar Hohokam territory and visits a Salado village. He lives with them for a while—perhaps because he became ill and couldn't return home to Mexico." His eyes grew hard. "Or maybe he fell in love with a local girl and couldn't bear to leave her. At any rate he lived with them long enough to have had some influence on their culture. When he died, they gave him an elaborate burial. It's all just conjecture, one possible explanation, but I'm sure your magazine editor will eat it up!" he finished cruelly.

She felt like she wanted to cry. She had been truly excited for him, for the significance the find might mean in his career. His cynicism about her interest in the event hurt. *It didn't matter what he thought of her anymore,* she tried to tell herself as she sat in the backseat next to Angelica. Nothing mattered anymore.

When they arrived at the ruin, Stacie took her own pictures of the newly exposed burial, feeling a little squeamish at the sight of the skeleton. But she managed some good photos of it and the remaining artifacts. The pendant had been brought to the safety of the archaeology laboratory, and she would have to photograph it separately.

She was asking Dr. Wilmott for permission to do this when he made the remark that there might be a great deal more important finds waiting to be uncovered. He wished aloud that Caldwell would let them have a full-scale excavation.

Stacie took the hint. Later in the day, Martin stopped by the ruin and he was obviously happy to see Stacie again. When he asked her to have dinner out with him that evening, she readily accepted.

"So you see how important it is that they be able to thoroughly investigate the ruin," she was saying as they were finishing their

Côtes d'Agneau Vert-Pré at an elegant French restaurant that evening. "Of course, it would be helpful for my article too" she added. She did not want to look as though she were trying to hide her own interest in the matter, though at this point she would have just as soon had her assignment over with so she could return to New York.

Martin smiled as he put down his wineglass. "Well, it's getting so I can't refuse you anything. I don't mind, Stacie. You can tell them tomorrow I agreed to it. I'll probably come by the ruin later in the afternoon as usual. I can discuss the details with them then."

She smiled broadly. "Thank you, Martin." She was surprised when he reached across the table and took her hand.

"I missed you while you were gone. I wish you had told me you were going on your trip. I probably could have arranged to come with you. You wouldn't have had to travel alone."

Stacie swallowed. "Well, I . . . it was kind of a spur of the moment decision. . . ."

He nodded. "And you're used to traveling alone. And you wouldn't have wanted to worry about what I would . . . expect." He watched tenseness enter her face. "I wouldn't have expected anything, Stacie. I've been trying to let you set the pace. But you won't be in Phoenix forever. Eventually you'll have to go back to New York and other assignments, won't you? I think it's time we made some assessment of our . . . situation."

Stacie inhaled deeply and suddenly felt guilty. She had never meant to lead him on, but it seemed perhaps she had.

"Now, Stacie, don't get nervous," he said with a smile, apparently reading her expression. "I know your divorce isn't settled yet. And I know you like me, but you're not . . . shall we say, head over heels about me. No let me finish," he said, squeezing her hand as she was about to speak. "Frankly, I'm not in the throes of deep passion either. Maybe I've got too old for that sort of thing. But I do feel comfortable with you; I like being with you, I admire your talent, and you're one of the most attractive women I've ever met. I like what we've got going, and I'd like to keep it up. And . . . if things between us continue to go smoothly, then . . . perhaps we can think about something more serious, maybe even marriage. But I wouldn't rush you. There's plenty of time. We both once made the mistake of rushing headlong into passionate love and it's given us broken marriages. I don't think either of us wants to make that mistake again. So, we'll take things slowly. Okay?"

Stacie wet her lips. She liked his gentle approach but had still been taken off guard. "If I have to go to New York, how would we see each other?" she asked, hoping to find some practical way to discourage him.

He smiled modestly. "I'm wealthy enough to afford frequent trips to New York or wherever your assignments take you. My foreman can run the ranch quite capably. You've told me part of the problem with your husband was your job. I assure you I would never interfere with your career, Stacie. I wouldn't want to see all your talent go to waste."

She lowered her gaze and felt the sting of tears at the back of her eyes. What wouldn't she have given to hear Gray say those words?

"Think about it, Stacie. You don't have to say anything definite now. We can discuss it again later."

She forced herself to smile and look up at him. "All right, Martin."

She did spend some time thinking about it that night before she fell asleep. Perhaps she would like to see him again when she was in New York. He was a kind friend to her if nothing else, and she wouldn't want to hurt him with an outright refusal. And perhaps one day, when she had got over Gray, if she ever did, she might want to form a more serious attachment to him. But that day was a long, long way off, and she didn't want to think about it anymore.

The next morning she went to the university as usual and found Gray in his office. No one else seemed to be around. He was sitting at his desk and looked up when she appeared at his door.

"Am I early?" she asked. "Where is everybody?"

"No, you're a few minutes late," he said, glancing at his watch. "Dr. Wilmott phoned me last night to say he won't be in today. His wife sprained her ankle and he wants to take her to the doctor."

"What about Tom and Angelica?"

"I called them and told them not to bother to come. I decided I'd like to work alone at the ruin—have some peace and quiet so I can think."

Tired of having Angelica chattering in your ear? she wanted to ask but didn't. "Why didn't you call me, then? I wouldn't have driven down," she said in slight irritation.

"You never gave me your phone number, darling," he said with airy sarcasm. "But as long as you're here, you might as well come."

"No, I wouldn't want to disturb you," she said, still annoyed.

"Far be it from me to keep an enterprising reporter from her work! Come on, let's go." He rose from his chair.

She was put off by his cold manner, but nevertheless walked with him to the Jeep. On the drive out they said little. Stacie's mind was engaged in comparing Gray's attitude about her work with Martin's. Her ruminating made her grow more and more sullen. Gray seemed to be preoccupied in thought too, but she had no idea about what.

When they arrived at the ruin, she had her usual problem climbing up the steep slope in front of the cave. She ignored Gray's offer to carry her equipment for her and managed on her own.

He went to work on the burial again, still carefully cleaning off dirt and dust from the fragile skeleton with a small brush, a trowel, and dental tools. He was sitting on the ground, his tall frame cramped in the confines of what remained of the walls of the small room. When he heard the click of Stacie's camera from the opening in the wall the archaeologists had made, he looked up. "You never tell me when to say cheese," he muttered humorlessly.

161

"I want to get you in a natural pose. . . ."

"Watch it!" he said sharply as she began to move closer. "Don't come in here. I don't want you stepping on anything."

"But I'd like to get a picture of the skeleton from a different angle."

"Hand the camera to me and I'll take it for you."

"You wouldn't know how to operate it properly," she retorted.

"Then you can use some of the photos I've taken, but I don't want you in here. One footstep in the wrong place and you could shatter something priceless."

Stacie had to smile. When they were first married she had been on digs with him and he had been the same way then. "No wonder Angelica was so put out with you," she couldn't resist saying. "Is that the way you talked to her?"

"It's the way I talk to anyone who doesn't know what they're doing."

"But I thought she was an archaeology student."

"She is, but she doesn't keep her mind on it."

"No, she's too busy flirting with her professor," Stacie said in a dry undertone.

Gray looked up and clicked his tongue derisively. "Still jealous, darling?"

Her carefully suppressed irritability suddenly frothed into a boil. "Will you stop calling me that! And I'm not jealous! If an immature girl with a big bosom and a big mouth is what suits your taste, all I can do is feel sorry for you."

"You're rather hypocritical, darling, since your taste seems to run to old men. How was your date with Caldwell last night?" he asked evenly, his attention still on his work.

She wondered if he had overheard Martin asking her to have dinner the day before. "Very nice," she snapped.

"Does he take you to expensive places?" he asked cynically.

"Sometimes," she replied, reining in her emotions. She wanted to be cool as she answered. "It's not why I let him take me out.

162

He's a gentleman, he respects me and my work, and I have a pleasant time talking with him."

She didn't like the way Gray chuckled. "Too old to do anything but talk, is he?"

She stared at his bent head as he continued to work. "That's very unkind, Gray. I should have told you, he's decided to allow a full-scale excavation here. I think you ought to speak of him with a little more respect."

Gray stopped his work and looked up. "He is?" he said with surprise. His dark eyes narrowed. "When did he decide that? Last night?"

"Yes."

Gray threw down the brush in his hand with a quick, whiplike movement. He was perfectly still as he looked at her with blackening eyes. "Why? How did you manage to convince him? You'd do anything for your damn magazine, wouldn't you?"

"What do you mean?" she asked, alarmed at his change of manner.

"You slept with him! Why else would he have given such a concession all at once? He's been breathing down your neck all these weeks. You finally gave in to him so you could get your story!"

"That's ridiculous! I wouldn't do any such thing! What would you care anyway?"

The fiery anger that was in his face abated a bit. His voice was cold as he reached for his brush again. "I don't! You're welcome to him!"

The words hurt. "Good!" she taunted back. "Because he's asked me to have an affair with him, and I probably will!" She was lying, but she didn't care. She wanted to wound him.

Suddenly his face was a deep color and his eyes flashed white hot. He got up and moved toward her. "The hell you will!" she heard in back of her as she turned to run away. The look in his face made her fear he would pull her apart limb by limb. She had run a few paces, nearing the steep slope, when she felt caught by two steellike arms around her rib cage. She struggled to get out

163

of his grasp, forgetting the delicate camera hanging from her neck.

"Let me go!" she screamed.

"How could you!" His voice was rough. "After what we had together! I'm the only one who knows how to make love to you! How can you go to him?"

"You've made it easy!" she said savagely. She struggled and twisted against his hold. He swore and his grasp loosened enough for her to escape him. She ran headlong toward the edge of the cave and the slope below.

"Stacie, no!" she heard Gray yell.

When she reached the edge she was afraid to slow up and stepped down onto the unfirm, rocky incline at the same speed, sure that her feet would not fail her now. With panic she saw the ground moving beneath her speeding legs at a dizzying rate. Then before she had realized it, her foot had slipped. She fell against the earth with a tremendous impact and continued to slide down, rolling over two or three times as she went, her camera thrown from her. Everything seemed a blur of rock and dust, and all she felt were hard, sharp edges hitting her body so quickly she could not react to the pain. All at once her sliding body slowed and then came to an abrupt halt in a cloud of dust.

"Stacie! Are you all right?"

She heard Gray's anguished cry, but all she could do was lie still. Her head was still spinning and a terrible pain at her elbow paralyzed her. She heard rushing footsteps and suddenly Gray was bending over her. She felt his hand on her forehead.

"Stacie, Stacie, are you hurt? Can you talk to me? Say something!" There was panic in his voice.

She wanted to, but there was dust in her mouth and the intense pain at her elbow made her whole body feel incapable of movement. A soft cry was all her throat could produce.

All at once he was on his feet again and she heard his footsteps hurrying away. She heard the Jeep door open and then shut a few seconds later. In moments he was back and throwing some rough, heavy material over her.

The pain was beginning to wane now, and she moved her hand to the throbbing elbow to rub it. She was glad that her bones felt firm under her touch. At least it wasn't broken, she was reasonably sure. She was trying to collect her wits, but all the while Gray's voice was assaulting her ears as he arranged the blanket over her.

"You stupid little thing! You never did know how to take care of yourself! You take chances and do things without thinking. You need someone to watch over you, don't you see that?" He bent closely over her face, touching her cheek with a trembling hand. She opened her eyes and looked into his.

"Are you all right? Can you see me?"

A faint smile came over her face. "Yes," she said weakly. "I think I'm all right. Just shaken up." She began to attempt to sit up, but he held her back.

"No, don't move. I'll drive to the ranch and call an ambulance."

She took her hand out from under the blanket and caught his wrist. "You don't need to. Let me try to sit up."

He looked troubled.

"Really, I think I'm all right," she insisted. "Let me up."

Reluctantly he released his hold on her shoulders. With her good arm she pushed herself slowly to a sitting position as Gray supported her back. The edge of the thick, wool blanket fell from her shoulders and into her lap. Her yellow short-sleeved blouse was disheveled and dirty.

"Are you all right?" he asked urgently.

"Yes, just my elbow," she said, rubbing it again. "I must have hit it against a sharp rock."

He inspected the injured arm. "It's beginning to swell a little, but I think it's all right. You've got cuts on your arms and hands, and one on your forehead," he said, touching each scrape. "You nearly scared me to death!"

"I was trying to get away from you. You looked like you were going to rip me apart!" she said, looking at his contrite face. He was several shades paler now.

"I was angry. I wouldn't have hurt you," he said softly.

"I know." Looking at his eyes she believed him. She took her gaze away from his face, for it touched her to look at him, and hurt her to know she was losing all that gentleness she loved in him. She looked down at the blanket still covering her legs. An odd little laugh that was mixed with tears escaped her.

"Gray, you're so silly. Giving me a blanket on a hot day!" She tried to keep her voice light so it wouldn't reveal her emotion. In one broad movement she drew the blanket off of herself and put it aside.

"I was afraid you might go into shock. You're too frail to take a fall like that. You could have broken your neck. For a few moments I thought you had!" he said as he brushed the dirt from her jeans.

She swallowed and tried to speak evenly, but her throat hurt with emotion. "Your problem, Gray, is that you've always been too protective. I'm a lot stronger than I look."

"No, Stacie." His voice had a strange, constricted quality. He lowered his eyes self-consciously and took his hands away from her. "My problem is that I've always loved you too much."

There was a weighted silence all about them in the dry, hot atmosphere. Somewhere overhead a bird flapped its wings in flight. She stared at his averted eyes. "Loved me?" she said, her voice barely audible.

He drew his wavering gaze to her face. "Of course," he said on a hush.

"You never said that before." Did he really mean it? she was asking herself feverishly, the green of her eyes suddenly looking as though lit from within.

"What do you mean? Of course I have." Though he denied her statement, color was flooding into his face under his tan. He couldn't look at her anymore.

"No you didn't, Gray."

"What difference does it make? You knew!" His tone carried both irritation and guilt.

"I was never sure. It would have made a lot of difference. I always thought . . ." She hesitated and he looked at her.

"That I just wanted you physically? How could you believe that? I thought it must be obvious to everyone how I felt about you! I was always so in love with you, it embarrassed me. Everyone must have taken me for a fool to be so hung up on a girl!"

"So you tried to be macho and not show it?" she said, touching his arm.

"I wasn't very successful," he muttered, eyes lowered.

"You were! I was never sure." An unexpected tear slid down her cheek. She hadn't realized she was crying. "Couldn't you have told me?"

He hesitated before speaking. "It's hard for me to say the words."

"Then tell me again . . . now."

He leaned forward and took her in his arms. "I love you!" he said in a passionate whisper as he held her close and pressed his mouth into her hair.

She put her arms around his neck and clung to him, her heart breaking with joy. Tears streamed down her cheeks and onto his shirt. "I love you too, Gray! I didn't mean what I said about Martin. I love you more than anything!"

His hands rose to her shoulders and tightened as he pushed her away a little to look in her face. "Then why don't you give up that damn job and come back and live with me?"

She could see he was trying to keep his expression firm, but there were tears in his eyes. It was impossible to refuse him. She knew she couldn't bear to leave him now. Leaning forward, she pressed her forehead against his chin. "All right, Gray. I'll give up my job. I'll be your wife again."

"For always? You won't be bored?" he pressed her.

"You'll have to let me have *some* kind of job," she said, looking up at him earnestly.

"Yes, but something here in Phoenix, and no long trips. I want you home with me!"

"All right," she agreed and then put it out of her mind. She

167

had him back again and that was all that mattered. A job was just a job.

He was enfolding her in his arms again, kissing her forehead. "We'll be happy, Stacie. I'll do everything I can to make you happy. I just want you with me. That's all I ever wanted."

His lips touched hers, reverently at first, then more urgently. She clung to him, returning his kiss with all her passion. The waiting fire quickly kindled between them and in moments he was gently pressing her back onto the ground. His hips to one side of hers, he leaned over her, kissing her face, her throat, then moving toward her breasts. He roughly unbuttoned her blouse and pressed his mouth into the soft swell above her lacy bra. Her hand was at the back of his head, urging him toward her. Laughing a little, she said, "Gray, not here," though the protest in the face of her actions was very weak.

"Why not?" he said, pulling at the material of the bra to expose her pink nipple.

She gave a little moan as his warm lips touched it. She forgot any further protests as his lips came back to her mouth and he relaxed the full weight of his chest upon her.

Their passions were reaching the point of no return when, dimly, she heard the sound of a motor. She tried to ignore it, but it kept getting louder.

"Gray," she said, shifting her lips from his. "Someone's coming."

He reluctantly pulled away from her and looked up as she heard the motor come to a stop close by. "It's Caldwell," he said irritably.

"Oh, no," Stacie murmured in alarm. She pushed herself away from Gray a little and began buttoning her blouse with hurried fingers. Roughly, Gray pulled her against him again.

A metal door slammed and suddenly Martin was standing in front of them. There was a hostile alertness in his countenance. "Stacie, what's going on here? Are you all right?" he asked, eyeing Gray threateningly.

"Listen, Caldwell . . ." Gray began.

"Gray . . ." she tried to interrupt, but he would not be silenced.

"Stacie is my wife, and I don't want you coming near her anymore!"

"*Your* wife!" Caldwell's widened eyes shifted to Stacie.

"It's true," she said. "I didn't tell you because I was afraid it would hinder work on the ruin. I'm sorry, Martin."

"But . . . I thought you were separated," Martin said, confused.

"We were. I thought we were getting a divorce, but . . ." She looked at Gray.

"We're not," Gray finished for her, looking at her with possessive eyes as he said it. He glanced up again at the rancher.

Stacie also lifted her gaze to Martin, afraid he would be angry or hurt. But Caldwell stood there with an introverted, philosophic expression for a long moment. "Well," he said at last, "I should have guessed it. I couldn't understand why you two were always so cold to each other. I'm happy for you, Stacie. Maybe passion *is* better." He smiled a little. Remembering their dinner conversation, she smiled back.

"You know, it may be for the best," Caldwell added. "My wife has been making overtures to me just lately—inviting me for dinner and that sort of thing. I never thought that would happen. If I'm lucky, maybe we'll be reconciling too."

"I hope so," she said, her mind instantly going back to Gray's chat with Mrs. Caldwell. She could see now that the flippant comments Gray had made were calculated to alert Mrs. Caldwell to take action, if she still had any interest in her former husband. Apparently she had.

Martin took a few steps closer. "How did you get so bruised, Stacie?"

"I slipped and fell down the slope," she said, her face reddening a little. "I'm okay." She hesitated. "Martin, will this make any difference about Gray's work at the ruin?"

The two men eyed each other for a moment. "No, of course not," Caldwell said. "I hope we can be friends. There was nothing between Stacie and me that you need to worry about, Gray.

I managed to hold her hand once, and that was about as far as I got," he said with wistful, self-deprecating humor. "You're very lucky."

Gray had risen to his feet. "I know," he said quietly and extended his hand to Caldwell.

When they had shaken hands, Martin said, "Well, I'll leave you two to go back to . . . whatever you were doing. I'll call my lawyer about drawing up papers for a complete excavation. See you later."

He turned to go, and Gray began helping Stacie up. As the rancher was driving off, Gray put her in the Jeep and then went back to collect her camera equipment.

"I'm sorry, Stacie," he said contritely when he returned. He placed a badly scratched camera with a shattered lens in her lap. "I'll buy you another to replace it."

While he was putting the rest of her equipment in the back, she examined it. It probably could be repaired, she was thinking. Poor camera. It had been a trusted workhorse for over two years.

But perhaps she wouldn't be needing it now, anyway. She probably could not get another job like the one she had. Especially not in Phoenix. If she was working for a local newspaper or somewhere similar, one camera would probably be adequate. Or maybe she would have to get some other type of job altogether.

She felt herself on the verge of a fit of depression, and consciously shook it off. None of that mattered, she told herself. If she had Gray she would be happy doing anything.

She handed the camera to Gray and he put it with the rest of her equipment. They drove off, a low cloud of dust behind the wheels as the Jeep took the bumpy ravine back to the gravel road.

"I think we should take you to a doctor, Stacie, just to make sure you're all right."

"I'd rather just go home. I'm okay."

"That elbow might have a cracked bone or something," Gray argued, glancing at her worriedly.

She smiled at him. "We'll see how it is tomorrow. I'd rather go home now and finish what we'd started before Martin came."

The expression in Gray's eyes changed and he grinned a little. "You *must* be feeling all right! But you're going to wash off those scrapes first when we get home."

"Yes, sir," she said dutifully.

In a while they had left the ranch road and were on the main highway back to Phoenix. The image of a buxom blonde kept appearing in Stacie's mind and she decided she'd better find out the truth.

"Gray, what about Angelica?"

He smiled and reached over to squeeze her forearm briefly. "You have no need to worry about her. I was trying my best to make you jealous, hoping somehow to get you back. So I pretended to be interested in her whenever you were around. Frankly, she's driving me nuts!"

"She told me she was having an affair with you," Stacie said, stoically pressing the issue.

He swiftly took his eyes from the road and looked at Stacie. "She what!"

"Said you were sleeping with her." She was relieved to see the astonishment in his eyes.

He muttered a few harsh, unrepeatable words. "You didn't believe her, did you? When did she say that?"

"It was one day at the ruin. She suspected there was something between us. I told her I was your wife, and that's when she said it. I thought she might be making it up, but I wasn't sure."

"She was lying through her teeth! I'm going to wring her neck next time I see her!"

"Frankly, I'd rather you didn't touch her, Gray," Stacie said with subtle amusement, directing a rueful glance out the window. "And you did lead her on, you know. I think she's in love with you."

"I guess it is my fault. She's been hanging around me for a long time. I should have known she would take my flirting seriously. My only thought was to try to impress you."

Stacie laughed. "I already knew you had co-eds chasing you, Gray! I was one of them. Remember?"

"Well, I just wanted you to know I haven't lost whatever it is that attracts them. I didn't want you to think I was pining away for you. . . . Even if I was."

"I thought you didn't like girls chasing you," she said, a trifle confused by his remarks.

"I don't. Though after you left me, it did boost my ego sometimes. I've never got involved with any of them—except for you."

She was thoughtful for a moment, recalling her student days. "Was I different from the others somehow? Why did you pick me?"

"You were very different. You behaved like a lady. Even when you were in my class, you didn't make any overt attempts to chase me. You were beautiful and shy, quiet and innocent."

Stacie was enjoying their nostalgic mood. "Did I disappoint you?" she asked a little sadly, reaching to stroke the denim material covering his thigh.

An odd look seemed to cross his face as she studied his profile. "You grew up. I can't blame you for what happened after we married. It was inevitable." His hand left the wheel and took hold of hers as she was touching him. "I'll try to keep you happy, Stacie. I know I'm . . . hard to live with. I wanted to keep you too close to me. I was afraid you were growing tired of life with me. I'm older than you, and . . . I'm not . . ." He left the sentence unfinished. "I'll try not to smother you this time, Stacie. Just . . . don't go too far from me."

She brought his large hand to her lips and tenderly kissed the smooth, tanned skin. "I won't, Gray. We'll make it work this time," she said, smiling up at him.

He kept his eyes on the road and said nothing more. There seemed to be a vague sense of gloom about him and she wondered why he was brooding again. Why now, when everything seemed to be going right?

CHAPTER ELEVEN

"Gray," she said, laughing as he put a wet washcloth to her face, "you're always fussing over me!"

They were at home in the bathroom off the bedroom. "That's why I married you," he said. He carefully dabbed at the small cut on her forehead. "So I could take care of you."

She was amused at that in light of his recent promise not to smother her. "I'm not that little girl you married anymore," she reminded him.

He was finished with her face now, having already taken care of the bruises on her arms, and tossed the washcloth into the wash basin. He leaned against the marble-topped vanity and looked at her thoughtfully, a hint of nostalgia hovering about his dark eyes. "I know. You're clever, talented, self-sufficient. A *fascinating* woman."

She smiled, a surprisingly shy smile for the woman he had just described. Stepping close to him, she lightly laid her hands against his denim shirt, feeling the warmth of his chest beneath. "I am?"

"Sure," he said, standing up from his leaning position as he clasped his hands at the back of her waist. "I never know what you're going to do next: kick me in the shin, throw a dirty quarter in my coffee, seduce me when I'm sound asleep."

He was smiling slightly as he spoke, deepening the attractive lines in his cheeks and at the corners of his eyes, and giving her a glimpse of his even, white teeth. Something made her reach up, glide her hand along his chin and then lightly tap his front tooth with her fingernail. In an instant he had caught the tip of her finger gently between his teeth and she playfully pulled it away. He looked down at her, his eyes warming with desire.

"Everything you do makes me want you more." He was leaning over her from his superior height and his breath warmed her cheek as he kissed her. Then he held her slender body close in his arms. "But part of me will always want to take care of you, darling. It's one thing about me you'll have to accept. To me you're still beautiful and frail and I can't help but want to protect you."

"I think I can live with that," she murmured softly, touched by the tender way he called her darling now. She kissed the warm, smooth skin beneath his open collar. Her hands went to his shoulders and then around his neck. She tilted her head back to look up at him and leaned her soft chest sensually against his, enjoying the feel of the warm pressure on her breasts. "Gray?" she said, her voice like a sigh.

The knowing glint in his eyes indicated he knew very well what was on her mind. "What?"

Her breath was growing a little uneven and her lips trembled slightly as she whispered, "Would you care to be undressed by a fascinating woman?"

His lips moved slightly to form a sensual smile as her hands moved to undo the heavy buckle on his belt. Slowly his large, beautifully formed hands moved from her back to the sides of her rib cage. His fingers trailed lightly over the small, demure mounds of her breasts toward the line of buttons at the front of her blouse. Beneath the thin cloth her skin tingled where he touched her and her breath began to come slightly faster in anticipation, the task she'd begun suddenly forgotten as he mesmerized her with his touch.

He started with the top button, then the second, which was positioned between her breasts. She closed her eyes for a moment, enjoying the light, prickly feel of Gray's fingers pulling at the cloth. As the material of the blouse parted, the gentle swells of her feminine form were exposed above the low-cut bra she was wearing. With a feathery touch he ran a forefinger over the lacy edges of the undergarment. As her breathing quickened and deepened in response, her swelling breasts rose and fell against his fingers, straining against the thin, transparent lace that held her soft flesh. The bra had a front fastening and she wanted him to undo it. Or rip the lace from her body, she didn't care! She wanted to feel the touch of his warm, moist lips on her bare skin.

But he hesitated, seemingly intent on taking his time, knowing from experience it would arouse her more. She almost wished he didn't know her so well.

As his hands moved to the lower buttons he gently took a step toward her, his thighs rubbing against hers as he urged her backward toward the open bathroom door. She smiled as he guided her through the door and she felt herself step onto the plush bedroom carpet. She had kicked off her shoes when she came into the house, and the soft woolly material felt good under her toes.

Finally he had reached the last button and pulled her blouse free of her jeans. With loving hands he pushed the garment off her shoulders and slid it down her arms. It fell to the floor, and Stacie was glad to be rid of it. She took his hand and guided it to her breasts, wanting him to caress her and remove the damn bra.

"Aren't you going to undress me?" he asked, an injured look in his eyes while a small smile hovered about his lips.

She smiled at her oversight. She had been so anxious to feel his hands on her, to continue and finish what they had started at the ruin, she had forgotten her provocative offer. Murmuring a little apology, she immediately began on the buttons of his

175

shirt. She had them undone in a matter of seconds and tugged the material free of his belt.

His tanned, muscular chest was exposed now. With a luxurious touch she ran her hands over his skin, beginning at the point of the V his soft, matted hair formed as it disappeared beneath his belt buckle. Her hands tingled and began to tremble a little as they passed over the flat abdomen and gracefully sculpted chest, grazing lightly over the nipples.

As her fingertips reached his shoulders she gazed up into his eyes. The playfulness that was there before was gone, replaced with a dark, brooding look of longing. She smiled, her eyes silently assuring him she was his, totally his. The dark eyes smiled back, but she still sensed hidden clouds somewhere in their brown depths.

Trying to recapture their more playful mood, her eyes took on a predatory gleam. She aggressively pulled the shirt off his shoulders and arms and tossed it aside. Her hands went to his belt, and she gazed up at him provocatively as she moved the stiff leather out of the brass buckle. Her fingers found the heavy metal snap at the waistband of his jeans. Her knuckles pressing gently into his stomach, she unsnapped it. She felt a responsive ripple in his abdominal muscles at her touch. With her fingers poised on the pull of the zipper she looked up at him again, brazen sensuality in her eyes. She was glad to see him smiling and looking devilish.

"Not so fast, woman! My turn again."

"All right, but let's hurry it up, mister!" she said saucily.

"I set my own pace!" he informed her.

As he took hold of her at the sides of her breasts, she smiled again mischievously. Coyly she placed her own hands over his. Then she pressed, and the heels of his hands pushed against her lace-covered flesh. She knew the action would bring out her cleavage to full advantage and it satisfied her immensely to see the raw desire kindling in his eyes.

He bent to kiss the soft swell of skin above one lacy cup edge. She made a soft, sensual sound in her throat at the hot, moist feel of his lips. His hands beneath hers seemed to grow warmer, and as he pulled them forward she felt his fingers beginning to tremble. He was moving more quickly now, to Stacie's relief, and his hands were slightly jerky as they manipulated the front clasp.

It was quickly undone. The fragile garment fell away from her feminine form, revealing lovely, rounded breasts and pert, rosy nipples. "All for you," she whispered warmly as she drew closer to him. His lips quickly found one little peak. The suction of his mouth and feel of his tongue on sensitive nerve endings thrilled her. She gasped convulsively and clutched the back of his head to press him closer.

"Oh, Stacie," he murmured with feeling, his lips moving to her other nipple, driving her wild. Her fingers caressed his hair and the sides of his face. But suddenly he straightened and was clasping her to him, crushing her against his chest.

"I love you, Stacie," he said, his voice at once tender and rough. "I love you! I couldn't bear it if you left me again."

"I couldn't bear it either, Gray," she said with emotion, her cheek pressed against his smooth shoulder. It troubled her that he still needed her reassurance. "I missed you so much, needed you, when we were apart. Many times I thought I had been a fool to have ever left you."

"I was the fool, trying to make you stay by threatening divorce," he said bitterly.

She looked up with a tiny smile, her eyes dewy. "But, you never went through with it. . . ."

"I couldn't." He pressed his lips to her forehead, as though she were something he worshipped. "I wanted to hope that you might come back. I thought about going to New York to see you. But when you never contacted me, except through that lawyer, I assumed you had forgotten what we had together, that you went on to something . . . someone better."

"There's no one better, Gray," she said, putting her arms around his neck, looking up at him earnestly. "No one better for me than you." She stroked his cheek. "Oh, Gray, let's not talk anymore right now. I want you to—"

Before she could finish, his mouth was on hers and he began drugging her with kisses and caresses. His ravenous mouth moved down her chin and throat. He bent his knees as his lips moved over her skin, lowering himself along her body, kissing every inch along the way, until he was kneeling in front of her. He pressed his cheek into her soft abdomen, his arms wrapped around her hips and upper thighs. He clung to her, and again she had that feeling of being worshipped. She bent over him, stroking his hair, murmuring his name. As she bent, her breasts grew full and pendulous. He stretched up to press his lips into the cushiony flesh, then kissed the firm hollow between her breasts.

She put her hand on his shoulders to balance herself as she kneeled in front of him on the floor. She turned tables then and clung to him, pressing her cheek against his chest, kissing his nipple. She felt his breathing quicken sharply and his heart began to beat hard beneath her ear. Knowing she was arousing him more and more, she continued kissing and licking until his hands grew urgent on her body. He had been gently fondling her breasts, but now with haste his fingers quickly moved to the waistband of her jeans. In one movement he ripped open the snap and zipper. He put his hands to her hips and pulled down the jeans, panties and all.

Gently but urgently his hands kneaded her soft derrière, then her outer thighs. They moved swiftly, softly, to the inside of her thighs, deftly caressing the smooth, sensitive skin. The sensation was making her wild. She felt his hand move upward.

"Gray, no, not yet! Take me to bed first! No more here." She said this in a whimpering voice into his neck. He paused to cradle her against him, then slowly stood up, pulling her shaking form up with him. When she was standing he pushed her jeans to her ankles so she could step out of them. When she had done so, he rose up again and she hurried to unzip his jeans.

When his clothes had been removed, the sight of his naked body made her breath catch in her throat. He was so strong and masculine, and, in arousal, so forceful looking. She had always felt a slight tremor of fear when she saw him this way.

As if he had read her passing emotion, he moved toward her and touched her face. "You aren't afraid, love, are you? I've always been gentle, haven't I?"

"Yes, Gray," she said, melting against him. "Always. But you look so . . . formidable. I feel helpless."

She heard him laugh lightly and looked up. "Good!" he said. "Because I've always felt helpless with you." He was urging her back toward the bed. "Helplessly in love," he murmured.

The backs of her legs touched the edge of the bed, and she eagerly let him ease her down upon the bedspread. She welcomed him into her arms, sighing with joy at the feel of his weight upon her.

Quickly he brought her again to the level of urgency she had experienced a moment ago when she had begged him to take her to the bed. His lips and hands followed one another over her throat, her breasts, her stomach, and thighs. She let him stroke her intimately then, his fingertips conjuring sensations that went to the very quick of her.

"Oh . . . oh, Gray," she softly moaned, dazed and clinging to him, too near the edge of her resistance.

Sharing her urgency, he moved upon her and they became one. They embraced in mutual, temporary relief. They were still for a moment, their bodies adjusting to a new plateau to climb. A languid, rhythmic movement began in their hips and thighs as their bodies molded to each other's, limbs entangled. He held her closely and she could barely breathe, his large, heavy frame encompassing her frail body. But Gray's overwhelming masculine essence around and within her made an exquisite confinement. She wished never to be released from it.

Her skin became dewy with a glaze of moisture as the movement between them created a new, awesomely unbearable tension. She knew she was on the verge of experiencing wild abandonment, that erotically frightening loss of control that Gray coaxed from her with such loving expertise.

And yet she did not want the pleasure she was experiencing now to stop. She loved the unbearable tension, loved the feel of him, loved what he was doing to her body. She liked being breathless in his embrace, enjoyed feeling his broad, masculine chest heaving with passion for her. She adored stroking and caressing his heated, surging body as it moved against hers. And the feel of him within her was exquisite.

She moaned softly in her inner dilemma, her breaths coming in small gasps to match his ragged breathing. His large body was shuddering now in the circle of her arms with each breath he took. It made her heady with power to feel the pleasure she was giving him along with her own. She writhed against him, stroked and kissed him, as he was doing to her. Only he knew she could be this way; only he knew this deeply sensual side of her. It made her secure and a little smug to know that of all the women who probably dreamed of loving him, she was the only one he took to his bed. She was the one he had married.

The mounting tension was at its peak now. She was gasping for air, and she could feel the shattering sensations within her that told her there was no more prolonging it.

"Oh, Gray . . . Gray!" she moaned, tightening her arms around him. For long seconds the tension was terrible in its power, like flood waters surging against a weakening dam. She stopped breathing, the air trapped in her lungs. Her eyes closed tightly as they shared the turbulent, triumphant moment. She felt as if she were tumbling through darkness, Gray along with her. A magic, mystical darkness.

After the monumental release, reality was slow to come back. Her body drifted into a narcoticlike relaxation in his arms. She lay against him, limp and spent. She felt him kiss her hair and murmur loving words. With a tender, contented smile, she lay her cheek against the damp hair on his chest and fell asleep to the gradually slowing beat of his heart.

Later Stacie was drying off with a heavy towel after stepping out of the shower. She heard the telephone ringing and quickly dropped the towel, went to the next room, and grabbed Gray's bathrobe from the bedroom closet. She reached the telephone on the bedstand while throwing the blue velour robe around her.

Gray had already showered and then gone out to get them something for lunch. They had discovered, to their mutual amusement, that they had forgotten to eat.

"Hello?" she said into the receiver as she sat on the mussed bed.

"Is . . ." there was a slight hesitance in the male voice, "is this Dr. Pierce's residence?"

"Yes."

"Is this Mrs. Pierce?"

"Yes."

"Stacie Smythe?"

She hesitated. Very few people knew her by both names, and she wondered who it could be, for the voice was totally unfamiliar. "Yes, that's my maiden name."

"Wonderful! I was calling your husband, but actually I wanted to talk to you." Stacie was mystified. "I'm Ron Hanover with *Southwest Scenes* here in Phoenix. Have you heard of our new magazine? The first issue won't be out for another six months, but we've been trying to get some preliminary publicity out."

"*Southwest Scenes,*" she repeated softly. "I may have heard someone mention it, but I really don't remember . . ."

"I don't imagine anyone at *American Traveler* is too worried about us threatening their market yet," he joked. "By the way, I'm very familiar with and admire your work. I knew who you were even before your husband showed me the magazine photos he had brought along."

"Gray?" she said, confused.

"Didn't he tell you? He came in a few days ago to see us. I think he said he had checked with the Photography Department at his university, and someone had given him my name. He said his wife was looking for a new job, one that would be in Phoenix and wouldn't require a lot of travel. When he heard about our new magazine, he thought it might be just what you wanted."

Just what *I* wanted! she was thinking. "So he came to see you?"

"Yes, and when I found out who you were I nearly fell off my chair. We've been hoping to get a photographer of your caliber and experience but figured we wouldn't be able to steal anyone away from a magazine like *American Traveler*. But as it turns out, your husband thought this might be the perfect job for you!"

Did he! she thought, her shoulders slumping and her expression growing morose. She listened quietly as he explained some of the specifics of the new magazine, its planned size and distribution, and what her job responsibilities would be. It was to be a scenic magazine of the Southwest and her travel would be limited to Arizona and its adjacent states. Also, he wanted her experience and knowledge to help get the magazine off the ground. She would have a higher position than staff photographer and writer. He asked her to come in for an interview so they could discuss her title and salary.

"I'd be happy to," she said politely, though she felt anything but happy at the moment. He named a day and time, and she agreed.

When she had hung up the phone, she remained where she was on the edge of the bed for several minutes, stewing about Gray's audacity. When she heard a car pull up she knew he had returned. Overlapping the big robe around her and cinching the tie belt tightly around her small waist, she left the bedroom to meet him at the door.

He laughed when he saw his large robe hanging from her small shoulders, but she did not smile back. She took the container of fried chicken he was carrying from him and walked into the kitchen. All the while her temper was building a reserve supply of steam. He followed her. When she had set the chicken down on the counter, she turned to him.

"I got a phone call while you were gone, Gray."

His eyes quickly surveyed the ominous signs in her too-steady eyes and tightened lips. "What's wrong?" he asked with concern.

"It was someone from *Southwest Scenes* magazine. I see you've arranged a job for me."

His eyes brightened and then dimmed again as he studied her grim face. "Well . . . it seemed like a great job—here in Phoenix, limited travel. I thought you'd like it."

"It's not your business to decide for me what I would like, Gray, especially without even consulting me! You're trying to manipulate me again, keeping me under your thumb by picking out a job that's okay with *you*. I resent that! You have to let me determine my own life. My life is not yours to manage, and I will not be a wife who's just an extension of you!"

The smooth angular planes of his face were growing taut. "All right, I'm sorry. I would have said something about it to you, but we weren't speaking much at the time. I hoped if things got better between us again and you knew this job was available, it might make a difference—it might make you more willing to give up the New York job. But since you willingly decided to give it up anyway, I'm sorry this happened."

"I still would have resented your interference, Gray," she said, trying to keep her patience. "You have to understand once and for all that I am my own person, an adult who's been working on her own for over two years. I don't need or want you to select a new job for me. I'm perfectly capable of doing that myself."

"I understand very well," he said in a brittle voice. "The truth is you don't need me for anything."

She glanced away, sighing impatiently. "Of course, I do!"

"For what? Sex?" he said. "You used to accuse me of treating you as a sex object. Actually, I'm beginning to think it's the other way around in this relationship!"

She looked up at him in astonishment. "That's ridiculous!"

"Is it? Women do, you know. I know I'm good looking. For years women have pursued me without any encouragement on my part. The more I ignore them, the harder they try. They see me in some romantic or sexual way that I frankly don't understand and don't want to. You were one of them, Stacie. So was that model I was so infatuated with years ago. She took one look

183

at me and decided she had to have me. The trouble was that after a while, she began to realize that my quiet, studious life-style didn't fit her image of what she thought I'd be. She must have wondered why such a handsome man didn't want to make entrances at parties, or why he wanted to study and work on his thesis instead of staying out all night with her. She cheated on me and strung me along, but I finally figured out what had gone wrong. She had just got bored."

Stacie listened to this uneasily, wanting to tell him they had got off the track—they were supposed to be discussing her job. And yet some instinct told her that what he was saying was pertinent somehow.

"I often wonder if Angelica and my other groupies got to know me better, had to live with me, how long they would stay," he went on. "I'm sure they would be disillusioned too. Like you were. You were so anxious to marry me, but after living with me for a few months you were bored out of your wits—except for the sex, of course. But even that wasn't enough. Your handsome professor had turned out to be dull and dusty and you couldn't wait to get away!"

Stacie felt deeply confused. "No, Gray. I . . . I didn't like being a housewife. I wasn't bored with *you*. But you wanted to keep me locked up here, under your thumb. And you're doing the same thing again by choosing a job for me!" she said, returning the conversation to the subject at hand.

"I thought that job was a good compromise!"

"How is it a compromise when I had no part in selecting it?"

"Refuse it then, if you like," he said tersely, putting his hands in his pockets and looking at the floor. "Keep your job in New York. If all I can have is part of you, I'll make that do." His voice had a hurt, sarcastic quality. "You can hop a plane back to Phoenix whenever you want to sleep with me."

She stared at him, transfixed. It was as if a veil in front of her eyes had been torn and for once she could see everything clearly. "Why do people get married?" he had once asked her. "Isn't it so they can be together every day?" The words had only confused her then. Now she understood what he meant.

She had been a fool. She had once lost what was most precious to her because of her own immaturity and self-preoccupation. And now she had nearly done it again.

She had never fully comprehended that it was Gray's insecurity rather than his lack of understanding or love that had made him so adamantly against her career years ago. Now he had gone out of his way to arrange what was actually a marvelous compromise, and she was still worried about the issue of control. The truth was clear as newly polished glass now: he didn't want to control her; he only wanted to feel sure of her love and know that she wouldn't leave him. Suddenly, she felt very free.

"Oh, Gray," she said in an endearing whisper of a voice, sorry now for all that had happened, for all that she had blamed him for, but had in truth been at least as much her fault as his.

He looked up at the sound of her voice, his eyes still darkly brooding and questioning. She moved toward him and put her hands lightly at his shirt collar.

"I'm sorry, I didn't understand," she told him. "I'll take the job in Phoenix, and I won't leave you. I'll try to do the traveling on weekends when you can come with me. And I won't be bored, Gray," she said, her mouth drawing into a smile. "I've never been bored with you! Don't you know by now that I adore being with you? I love to watch you think and work. Even breathe."

He lifted his eyebrows in a quizzical movement. "Are you sure? I thought you had outgrown what you saw in me when we married."

"Not in the least! I love your moods, I love your character, I love your gentleness. And I love your sexy body and the way you use it, but don't ever think that's all I love. I shouldn't have taken that assignment in Alaska. I should have waited for something else. . . ."

"No, Stacie. It was a wonderful opportunity. It made your career. I was so proud of you when *Southwest Scenes* knew who you were at once. I didn't have to sell you at all. It was just that years ago I was afraid if you left you would find someone you liked better, or go away and . . ."

"Never come back," she finished for him. "I misunderstood it all. I just thought you had turned male chauvinist. I paid for it though," she said, tears forming in her eyes. "I was never happy away from you. It was only my job that kept me going."

He nodded. "It was the same with me. Only after a while I was even losing interest in my work. We're a pair, aren't we?" he said with a broken laugh. He put his arms around her and hugged her tightly. "Oh, Stacie," he said, his lips in her hair at the side of her face, "for once I feel genuinely happy! I've been just existing for years, even before I met you. The few months we were together were the only happy time I can remember since I've been an adult. Now it'll be that way again!" He drew away a little and looked down at her, smiling. "For the rest of our lives." The amber highlights were glistening in his eyes and his face had no trace of that somber quality she had seen so often.

"You mean you're going to stop brooding?" she said, trying to tease him by looking disappointed.

His shoulders shook as he laughed and she saw more teeth than she had ever seen when he smiled. "I may," he said.

"What'll I do?" she quipped, captivated by the sound of his laughter.

His smile dimmed slightly and the look in his eyes changed. Their dark, suggestive glint sent an overpowering tremor through her. "Seduce me?" he suggested.

She swallowed before she could speak, and her voice was like a breathless hush. "Now who's only interested in making love?" she said, the green of her eyes seeming to deepen as her lashes grew heavy with desire.

He looked at her knowingly, his voice caressing and intimate. "At the moment, I think we both are . . . my darling."

LOOK FOR NEXT MONTH'S
CANDLELIGHT ECSTASY ROMANCES ®

A cold-hearted bargain...
An all-consuming love...

THE TIGER'S WOMAN

by Celeste De Blasis
bestselling author of *The Proud Breed*

Mary Smith made a bargain with Jason Drake, the man they called The Tiger: his protection for her love, his strength to protect her secret. It was a bargain she swore to keep...until she learned what it really meant to be The Tiger's Woman.

A Dell Book $3.95   11820-4

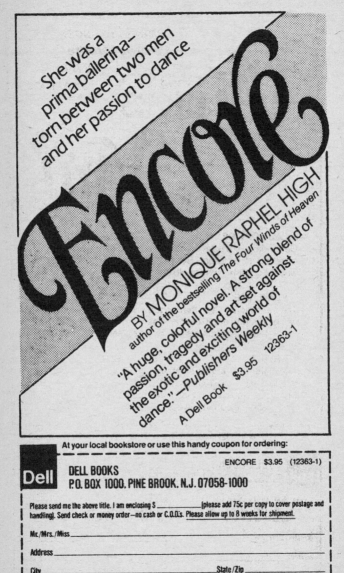